GRIMDARKE

THE MAW OF MAYHEM MC
BOOK 1

AK NEVERMORE

KEEP READING AFTER THE BOOK TO GRAB

The Maw of Mayhem

A **FREE** MAYHEM NOVELLA PREQUEL

———

Cover design by BookMojo

Print ISBN: 979-8-9887464-2-3

Digital BIN: 011053-03596

TABLE OF CONTENTS

DEDICATION

This one is for Paigery, my inner voice when shit hits the fan. Love you, cuz.

CONTENT WARNING

Don't try this at home and a heads up: This book explores themes which some readers may find uncomfortable or offensive. If violence, smut, various kinks, salty language, drug use, and generally unsavory behavior are triggers for you, please put this novella down and back away slowly.

BEFORE

BASS THUMPED, heavy and hot, throbbing up through the soles of Grim's shit kickers. The club's black lights flickered with the beat, highlighting the sweat-slicked bodies undulating in a writhing mass of lust and abandon below him.

He leaned back against the balcony's bar, vibing enough "don't fuck with me" to keep all but the brain-dead sluts off him. Not that he could blame them, but he didn't tend to stick his dick in stupid. Or anything else.

—laughing—

Happy about that, you furry motherfucker?

Fucking cat was out of control. Grim scanned the pit of simmering sex below, the stink of human desire thick in his nose. He turned to his alpha, not fucking impressed, or in the mood for bullshit. "This is what we rode five hours for?"

Clay gave a slow nod, more close-lipped than usual, totally fixated on one of the Lucite pillars rising from the dance floor. Grim shook his head and took another sip of his overpriced beer. Clay'd spill when he was ready and not a moment before. There had to be a damned good reason for them to be there, and if he wanted to stare at an empty platform, more power to him. The others had plenty of eye candy to enjoy.

And human or not, those dancers could move, their

getups not leaving much to the imagination. Fishnets, booty shorts, and shredded Ts reading "Skin" straining across their tits as they worked the poles in the center of each platform.

But as much as he approved on principle, his dick couldn't care less.

[SMUG]

Fuck his cat and this shit. He downed the last of his beer and cracked the glass onto the bar. "Gotta piss."

Grim shouldered past, and Clay grunted, still fixated on that platform. Whatever had caught the alpha's attention had brought his cat close to the surface. He wasn't going anywhere.

Grim pushed through the crowd, shrugging off roaming hands and bodies pressing close. Whispered promises and innuendo fell on deaf ears. One brazen stolen kiss, and a tongue laced with the tang of a narcotic tangled with his. He spun the woman back into the throng and spat.

Hall for the john was packed, moans coming from the men's room. He shouldered past the line for the ladies', through the door.

"Hey! You can't—"

Yeah, he could. A dozen stalls, all closed. Wide eyes watching him in the mirror, lipstick and mascara dropping, their owners scurrying back like vermin, gasping as he unzipped and started pissing into the sink. Grim's head tipped back with a long exhale. *Fuuuck—*

A flush and slam of a stall door opening. The water in the sink beside him crashed on. He glanced over. A petite, raven-haired woman dressed like the podium dancers beneath a man's oversized, unzipped hoodie soaped up her hands. Grim pursed his lips at her sinful curves. God freaking damn...

"You know that's not a urinal, right?" she asked, her reflection glaring at him in the mirror.

Or more accurately, glaring at his cut.

Her whiskey-dark eyes flicked up and met his. Grim's mouth went dry. His dick twitched as he shoved it back into his jeans. She didn't drop her gaze. "Desperate times." Grim's voice rumbled, his inner beast sitting up and taking notice, along with his cock. *Are you fucking kidding me?*

—want—

Now you want? He barked out a laugh. The shit on that chick's tongue must've been a premium grade miracle.

Little miss five-foot-nothing-and-not-into-bikers reached past him to slap on the water in his sink, rinsing it down. "That's fucking disgusting. You need to leave before I call security."

Damn, she was a live one.

Grim crowded into her space, and she didn't budge, glaring up at him with her hands on her hips, just begging for him to smack that ass. He wet his lips and stroked down the side of her cheek, trailing to her quickening pulse. Her hand snaked up to grab his wrist, and a jolt went through him, cock kicking against his zipper.

The ebony of her pupils blew out, eating away the warmth of her irises. The scent of her arousal flooded his nose. Her breath caught, then stuttered out, a little crease appearing between her brows. "D-don't touch me."

"Stop wanting me to," he murmured, tilting up her mouth to his.

Her fist took him in the jaw, and he stumbled back. The fuck?

—YESSS—

Within, his beast coiled to pounce as she flung open the bathroom door, storming out—

Gunshots.

Clay.

Grim's cat scrabbled to get out. The beast's consciousness slammed into his, overwhelming him with the desire to shift and charge through the crowd, rending and tearing until he—

The hallway erupted with people frantic to escape, and the woman fell back into the bathroom. He lunged forward to steady her, the press of her body against his distracting the beast long enough for him to wrestle back control. She wriggled away, and Grim slammed the door shut and locked it, panting.

Shit, that was close…

[ANGER]

We're not shifting here. He needed to think, not react, Goddamn it. He pulled his cell, then shoved it back into his pocket. Fuck. They'd ridden down alone. MC wouldn't be able to back them up for hours. He raked a hand through his shaggy blond hair and pulled his piece, listening for a break in the deluge of bodies streaming past the door.

Movement to his right. The woman had flattened herself against the far wall. Grim rocked his jaw. She had one hell of a hook, and a set of legs to match. Damned if they weren't tight as fuck…

"Don't even think about it, asshole," she gritted out, eyeing his gun.

Grim smirked, shifting his cock. Oh, he was thinking about it, all right. Her peaked nipples and the way she rubbed her thighs together said he wasn't the only one.

—Clay—

Right. Wasn't the fucking time. Head in the game. The rush outside the door had dissipated, and Grim raised his gun, fingers on the doorknob. He glanced back at her.

"Stay here."

She rolled her eyes, arms crossed over what had to be all natural DDs.

Goddamn.

—want—

Later. He unlocked the door and eased it open, then slid—

She burst out from behind him and was gone before the door slammed against the wall. A smile tipped up his lips, his proverbial tail twitching. Any other situation, he'd chase that down and tag it. Fucking figured he and his cat would agree on something now.

The hall was deserted, a lone cocktail napkin fluttering abandoned in the pulsing lights. Grim's jaw clenched, the shit music drowning out any sounds from the balcony above. His finger inched toward the trigger, the dusky scent of cat edging out the reek of humanity in the room.

Mother. Fucker.

He crept up the stairs to the balcony—

"I done told you what would happen, Claymore, laying rights on what ain't yours to claim. Destiny always takes its due."

Grim's foot paused on the last step, his stomach dropping at the gravelly deep woods drawl. No—Asshole had close to four more years in the pen—

"Fuck you." Clay gritted out, his voice racked with pain.

"Mmm, think I'll fuck that ol' lady of yours instead. Heard Marie ain't much for conversatin' these days, but I ain't never been real interested in what she had t'say."

Grim ducked into an alcove behind the curtain of the VIP section. Swearing and a scuffle sounded over the pounding techno beat, then the sharp crack of flesh on flesh.

Man laughed at Clay's agonized groan. "Easy… knock that blade free, an' you'll ruin the scene. Let's stretch this out a tick. Shiv, kill that Godawful shit."

A semi-automatic fired and the music cut out, the silence a deafening void.

Grim nosed the dusky velvet curtain aside with the barrel of his gun, peeking through. Cold sweat drenched his body, cat trying to tuck tail. He fought to kill the whine scrabbling to burst from his insides. Wishing like hell his eyes hadn't confirmed what his churning guts already knew.

Reaper was out.

[FEAR]

Yeah. They were fucked. Totally fucking fucked.

Across the room, a half dozen brothers from their rival MC, Satan's Vengeance, were raiding the bar with one eye on the show. Grapple, Reaper's enforcer, had Clay on his knees, one massive hand ripping the alpha's head back to bare his throat.

The other was on a silver knife buried to the hilt in Clay's shoulder.

That son of a bitch.

Grim swallowed bile, shoving away the memory of that burn. Black fire webbing decay through his flesh, paralyzing his beast—

—run—

No. Let me think. Shit was easier said than done, but— how'd they know to hit them at the club tonight?

Unless the MC had a rat… or a Mouse. Fucking tech nerd was supposed to be keeping tabs on the prison. Anger stilled the tremor in Grim's hand, and he blinked the sweat from his eyes. Because if Reaper and his brothers were here, they hadn't just been betrayed by one of their own, they'd been offered up on a silver fucking platter as sacrifices.

How the hell had the psycho prick gotten out?

The lanky biker sniffed, running a hand under his nose. Grim tensed at the smirk tipping up the asshole's lips, keenly aware of the stink of his own fear. Reaper snagged a bottle from one of his boys. His rings clanked against the glass as he imbibed, that icy blue gaze, dead as skittering leaves, sweeping the shadows—

—until it met Grim's.

Reaper's lips twitched again. "Ah. Now that we're all here—"

He raised his gun and blew away half of Clay's skull.

CHAPTER ONE

UPSTATE NEW YORK in the fall was beautiful, and it made Kit want to puke.

She gripped the steering wheel tighter, her sweaty palms slicking the leather, and glanced in her rearview, then at her phone's GPS. No service—again. Damn it. This was not where she wanted to be…

Wait. Signs for a trailhead were coming up. *Thank you, sweet baby Jesus.* She pulled onto the shoulder, staring blankly at the plexi-covered map tacked onto the tiny shelter in front of the car. Woodbine Swamp Trail. Shit. She'd missed the turn-off for the house. Ugh! How could everything in this shit town look the same and so frickin' different all at once?!

Fifteen years will do that, genius.

Her forehead dropped to the steering wheel, bumping it thrice. Stupid. Stupid. Stupid. She couldn't do this. She couldn't—

Goddamnit, girl, grow a pair!

Enough. Wasn't like she had a choice. She pushed back in her seat and slapped the car in reverse, hoping like hell there wasn't anything behind her. Frickin' hatchback was stuffed to the gills with the sad remains of her life, and she wasn't up for losing any more of it.

Kit dashed away a tear. And whose fault was that?

She just had to blow shit up. Couldn't duck her head and

keep punching numbers, because "lay low" was too big of a fucking ask. Nope, fuck overtime at the accounting firm, had to go out there and twerk her ass at the club, knowing full well that milkshake wasn't gonna bring anything but trouble to her yard.

Her mind leapt to that tall drink of golden Viking god pissing in a sink, covered in tattoos and oozing temptation. Yup. Case in point, and as much as it shocked the shit out of her, she'd been into him.

So fucking into him, like, wanted him into her.

Not happening.

She bit at a cuticle, trying to ignore the very real possibility she was about to deliver herself to his doorstep, and the fact that her panties had just soaked clean through.

Son of a—Chanté would quip something about chickens coming home to roost, but they weren't even Kit's damned chickens. And why the fuck chickens? Woman was NYC born and raised, you'd think she'd have useless witticisms about pigeons.

Damn, though. He was fiiine…

Stop it.

You'd think she'd be more concerned about the shifter shadowing her for the past two weeks… the one whose face starred in her nightmares. Reaper hadn't approached her, but his message was clear, and like a fucking cat, he'd been playing with her.

… Run, little mouse…

Kit's teeth clenched at the memory of her father's gravelly twang. She put the car in gear and kept driving in the wrong direction. Away from the house, toward the last damned place she wanted to go, and the only place she had left. Two weeks of couch surfing and shitty motels had made that abundantly clear, and her flat fucking broke.

Back to the scene of the crime, the one place she hoped like hell he didn't have the balls to go back to.

Motorcycles rumbled in the distance and her gut threatened to rebel, cold sweat pebbling her skin. She licked the anxiety from her lips.

The rumble grew, and a moment later a stream of leather and exhaust whipped by her as a convoy of bikes sped past, heading back toward civilization. A manic giggle burbled from her throat, and she took a slow—

Shit! Gas pedal, girl, you gotta keep your shit together…

Focus. Drive to the damned compound. One more mile.

… And keep it together. Hah! Fat fucking chance. She blew out a breath, her temples thudding with the beginnings of a migraine. Goddamn. After all those years of praying to be out from under Claymore James's thumb… this had not been part of the fantasy.

Getting shit-faced, twerking on his grave, and then setting the MC's compound on fire, yes. Pulling up to the chain-link gate and asking to see Mud Knuckle?

Nope. Can't say that'd made the list, but here she was.

I mean really, Mud Knuckle? Kit sighed, rubbing a temple. If she needed any further confirmation her life had officially gone to shit: Ta-frickin'-da.

One of the dopey-looking prospects manning the gate eyed her, pursing his lips. The scraggly little pornstache he was rocking made his mouth look like a porcupine's asshole.

Moron leaned in her window. "Ain't no muddy knuckles here." He snickered, shooting his zit-infested buddy a look.

Kit sighed. Great, they were gonna fuck with her.

"Nah," Zits said, ambling closer to leer. "But I ain't opposed to rectifyin' that situation." He grinned, making a lewd gesture.

Whoo. Ten points for originality there, son. She rolled her eyes and unbuckled her seatbelt. It was showtime. The two high school rejects scrambled back, wide-eyed when she threw open the door and got out, leaving the hoodie she'd permanently borrowed from Chanté on the seat. Fuck, it was hypothermia cold.

"What? I thought we was 'wreck-t-fyin' that sits-e-ate-shon,'" she finger quoted, mimicking his dipshit twang and cocking a hip.

Pornstache's throat bobbed, taking in her tight tee and yoga pants. God, men were pigs. Pathetic, predictable pigs. Flash them braless DDs, and their brains shorted out faster than a hairdryer in a bathtub. Add the fact that her nipples were hard enough to cut glass, and the poor boys didn't stand a chance.

"Uh, yeah." Pornstache tugged on his cut and cleared the squeak from his throat. Slack-jawed, Zits smacked his shoulder, earning himself a glare. "I mean, hell yeah. We're down, baby."

Kit arched her back, stretching. Damn, that felt good after five hours behind the wheel. Pornstache groaned like he was about to wreck-t-fy in his pants. She sauntered over and ran a finger down his sternum.

"Then how 'bout you boys open the gate so I can move my car out of the way and get down to business."

Zits moved so fast he just about face-planted rushing to unlatch the big chain-link section on wheels blocking the compound's access road. He'd pulled it halfway across the pavement by the time Kit got back into her car. Pornstache shook his head like a dog, blinking as the door clunked shut, and he stumbled over to help his buddy.

Suckers.

Kit almost felt bad as she drove past, waggling her fingers.

Okay, no, she didn't. She wriggled back into the hoodie, one hand on the wheel and shivering. Her stomach churned as she drove around the last bend to the chapter house, half expecting the entire club to be out there waiting for her. The woods opened up—

And the lot was empty.

Of frickin' course it was empty. The funeral was today. Now. She could still make it. Wasn't that why she'd blown out of the city so fast? To spit on Claymore's grave like she'd told Chanté she was going to? Get some kind of fucked-up closure?

Yeah, has nothing to do with the fact you're being stalked by a psycho.

Kit bit back a sob, coasting the last few hundred feet to a stop in front of the long, two-storied building. It was ugly. A dark, cinderblock gray, squatting against a barren hillside. She bit her lip, eyes flicking to the last window on the left, waiting for the shitty mini blinds to part.

They didn't. Wouldn't.

Dead. Everything looked fucking dead. Probably because it was.

Fuck this shit. She jerked up the emergency brake and killed the engine. Slammed the door open, then shut. Stomped across the half-frozen muddy lot, odd bits of gravel and glass crunching beneath her boots. Eyes fixed on the burnt-out jaws scored into the surface of the MC's chapter house door, she approached the belly of the beast—

—And stepped into the Maw of Mayhem.

———

Grim stood beside an open grave, looking anywhere but at the casket.

Low fieldstone walls. Tumbled tombstones green with lichen and pitted with age, the epitaphs worn smooth. Craggy, unkempt trees jagged their roots out like lightning between monoliths and statuary, skewing the cobblestone path akimbo. And in the far corner, a small chapel with arched, diamond-paned windows. It hunched half-hidden in a copse of trees, its brick-red cathedral-style door slightly ajar, taunting him with what was inside.

Nah, check that. More like threatening him with a who.
[ANGER]
Fuck her.

Sights seen, he raised his flask, wrists still scabbed and swollen, ribs aching, numb to the burn as he swallowed. Goddamn, it was a shit day to bury someone.

—whimpering—

Cold. Wet. Standing in mud up to his asshole. The smell of dead leaves, pending snow, and wood-burning stoves scraping down the back of his throat. Stinging his eyes—he shot a hand across his face and pinched the bridge of his nose.

Fuck. Keep telling yourself that's why you're tearing up, you pussy. Sure as hell wasn't the shit sermon he'd just sat through, and the priest's sanctimonious second act graveside wasn't any better. Fucking civ.

His sonorous drone alone deserved a beatdown. Prick wasn't even attempting to veil his contempt. You'd think a man of God would have more tact, or at least more sense. The graveyard was a sea of leathers. There had to be close to two hundred patches crammed in graveside. The white-on-black fanged Maw of Mayhem was predominant, but plenty of cuts from associate MCs were in attendance, and the atmosphere was dense with grief and some seriously dank bud.

Shit, maybe that would chill his cat the fuck out. Whiskey sure as hell wasn't, and his inner beast was moodier than a teenaged girl.

"… through our Lord Jesus Christ, we commend to Almighty God our brother Nathaniel *Claymore* James…" The priest's tongue curdled around the name. Motherfucker was just asking to get hit—

—YESSS—

Grim's hackles rose, fur bristling from his nape. Goddamn it. *No. Not fucking here, and not fucking now.* He shoved the beast back down, spinning from the grave and stalking to the edge of the crowd. Brothers gave him a wide berth and curt nods as he passed, their ol' ladies laying on the sympathetic moues, inevitability in their eyes.

Just waiting for him to lose it.

Grim gritted his teeth, trembling hand scraping back the hair from his eyes. He wasn't gonna lose it, and he didn't want their fucking pity.

What he wanted was for his alpha—damn it, his fucking father—not to be rotting in a Goddamned box. Short of that, he'd take doling out the same fate to the asshole that put Clay in there, and this fucking circus wasn't getting him any closer to that goal.

Not that he'd been able to pull the trigger when he'd had a chance.

The memory of Reaper's alpha command paralyzing him while his brothers beat the shit out of him spiked rage-fueled fear up Grim's spine, making him hyperaware of every lingering contusion.

Why the fuck hadn't they ended him?

From the side-eye he was getting, he wasn't the only one that wanted to know.

"… though we are sinners, you wish always to hear us. Accept the prayers we offer in sadness for your servant Nathaniel *Claymore*…"

[ANGER]

A growl rumbled through Grim's chest. That was it. Priest was about to be introduced to his own hole in the ground—

A hand clamped down on his shoulder. Stitch. The club's sergeant-at-arms' rheumy oyster gaze bored into him, his voice a low rumble. "That priest ain't worth losing it over, and we got a situation."

Grim shrugged out of his grip. "No shit, and I'm fine."

"Bull." Man snorted, heating up his vape. "And I ain't talkin' about this clusterfuck. Them two chuckleheads we left manning the gate let some chick in."

"They stupid?" Grim dragged a hand down his face. Dumb question.

"She asked to see MK."

"What the fuck does she want to see Mud Knuckle for?"

Stitch took a hit, lips thinning as he held it, and shrugged. "Dunno." He exhaled. "But hear tell she was hot as hades, mid-twenties, and her car was crammed full of shit. Maybe another one of his by-blows comin' home to roost?"

Great. Grim pounded the last of what was in his flask. Because the first one that'd showed up was such a fucking prize.

Stitch chuckled for all the wrong reasons. "Nikki's a snake, but tell me you ain't thinking about a sister sandwich. Fuck, if this one's as hot as her—"

"I'm not. After all the shit she's pulled—"

"Whatever, kid. We both know that for better or for worse, that pussy's got you whipped. You know my money's on worse, but that ain't here nor there." He frowned, rubbing his forehead. "Peel off. Go get your dick sucked. She's around, ain't she?"

Grim glanced at the chapel. Yeah, she was here all right, wanting to cash in on their deal. He just wanted it to end. Stitch was spot-on about her being a snake. She'd slithered back into the club's good graces with some bullshit Come-to-Jesus act while Grim'd been laid up the hospital, claiming they'd made amends and acting like his queen. Jesus fuck, his father's body wasn't even in the ground. Dealing with her shit was the last thing he wanted to do.

"Fuck her," he muttered.

Stitch's eyebrow rose as he cleared his carb. "I ain't gonna hold my breath on that count. Else you woulda come clean to the club about your deal with her already. Ask me, it's high time you do. Clay's in that box yonder. Ain't nothing you confess is gonna hurt him."

Grim kicked at a chunk of frozen mud. Maybe not, but

Stitch didn't know all the details. Nikki did, and her spilling had the potential of planting Grim right beside Clay.

"You know," Stitch mused, "She's sportin' a bite. Says it's yours. One way or another, you need to address the shit she's pullin', quick."

Fucking manipulative—Bite wasn't his, not that he could publicly dispute it. Grim jammed his hands wrist deep into his pockets, wishing he could smack her shit down, but the bitch had him by the balls and liked to yank.

Stitch sighed out his hit. "Christ, at least go for a run. You gotta let that beast of yours out."

No shit, and the thought of pounding through the mountains on four paws—

[JOY]

—but fuck, add it to the Goddamned list of shit he had to deal with since Clay'd been executed. Grim scratched his bristled jaw.

"Priority's not on my dick or a run, it's making Satan's Vengeance pay."

The old man took another hit and inspected the tip of his vape. "Gonna be pretty hard to take out an entire MC if you're all by your lonesome. Nikki's shit aside, way it went down with Clay… brothers want answers I know you ain't keen to give."

Grim looked away. "I told 'em what happened."

"Yeah, but not the why."

"Why the fuck does Reaper do anything?" he snarled, getting in Stitch's face. "He left me breathing to fuck with people's heads." Including Grim's. That Goddamned alpha command forcing his obedience… How the hell was he gonna lead the MC if another alpha could bend him over with a word?

Which meant Reaper wasn't done with him—not by a long shot.

Stitch didn't bat an eye. "You're alive 'cause you're his kin.

Man's a sadist, no argument there, but nepoticide ain't in him."

"Don't be so sure about that," Grim muttered, wincing at the lancing pain through his ribs and hating himself for it. "And he's not my uncle."

Stitch snorted. "Maybe not by blood, but he loved Abigail somethin' fierce. Was a damned tragedy the way him and Clay fell out over your mama. Her dying broke the both of them... Fucking broke us all." He took another hit off his vape and glanced at Grim askance. "Some more than others."

Grim tensed and Stitch doubled down. "It's past time you came to an understandin' with that bitch-ass beast of yours and set all this shit rollin' down the hill to rights. You're as alpha as Clay was. Time to own it and kick that bitch Nikki to the curb."

How high was the old man? Grim and his cat understood each other just fine. He did his thing, and the furry fucker dealt with it... most of the time. He shook his head, not wanting to get it.

Stitch didn't seem to notice, or more like didn't care. "And that means coming clean, about *all* of it."

—the concrete room was ice-cold, dark brown ridges of offal frozen to the gritty floor. His tongue scrapes at it, torn and weeping, broken claws scrabbling for something, anything, to fill the gnawing void in his belly. The steel door clangs open, and a molly saunters into the room yowling, tail high and pitched to the side—

Fur bristled at Grim's nape, and Stitch grabbed him by the scruff, staring him down. "And you need to do it soon. The shit that hit the fan when Clay manned up and claimed you as his son ain't gonna be dick in comparison, and if they figure out how close you are to goin' feral again... They'll hunt you the fuck down, and he ain't here to save your ass."

[GRIEF]

The beast retreated, and Grim growled, shrugging loose. No way was he ready to throw his PTSD on the table for everyone to paw through. Wasn't happening... unless Nikki spilled it. Grim swallowed his fear, needing more time. As long as she thought she was gonna be his queen, she'd stay mum.

And if she didn't?

Grim toed a gravestone.

"... May his soul and the souls of all the faithful departed, through the mercy of God, rest in peace. Amen."

Thank fuck.

The rumbled response of the crowd signaled the end of the service, and brothers started vying for Grim's eye, either to offer their condolences or assess his mental state. The first he didn't want, and the second would be fine, right after he personally put a bullet in each and every member of Satan's Vengeance, starting with Reaper.

And on that note...

"I gotta get outta here," he said to Stitch, eyeing the chapel door. "Gonna run back to the clubhouse—"

[JOY]

"—grab the Indian and check out how deep MK's dick has got us in it this time."

Stitch grunted, slapping Grim's shoulder. "Clay'd like you takin' her out, but don't get lost. Ride starts in an hour. Club's gonna expect you to show and say some words about the man."

"Right." Grim turned away, gut clenching like he was gonna puke.

He kept his eyes glued to his boots on the way out of the cemetery. Say some words. What the fuck did they expect him to say? His father was dead. Shot in the face by a psycho prick that had Grim by the short hairs and the rest of the MC by extension.

Fuck.

He smacked the side of the cage Clay had taken his final ride in and shucked off his cut, thumbs running over its patch. *Boo-fucking-hoo, asshole. Suck it the fuck up.* Grim sighed. He should be grateful.

He should be dead.

Clay'd saved him, given him that first chance when he pulled him out of Reaper's basement, and then another after Grim's cat had fucked that up by going feral. He owed it to the man not to waste this one, needed to honor his memory, keep his shit together, and do this, 'cause Stitch was right—he was on thin fucking ice.

Grim sniffled, pinching the bridge of his nose. Goddamn smoke. He tore off the rest of his shit and tossed it into the hearse. One of the brothers would make sure it got back to him. His body ached—a mottled collection of color courtesy of his fucking "uncle" and the two shitheads he'd shared a womb with. The memorial ride was gonna be literal hell on wheels for his ribs.

Good. He fucking deserved it. He dropped to hands and knees, hissing back pain as joints popped and muscles shifted from his human form into that of a mountain lion. Colors bled from the landscape and the distance softened to a blur. Sounds multiplied and sharpened.

[JOY JOY JOY]

A fragrance teased his nose.

He sneezed. Shook his head. What the hell was that? His lips curled up over sharp canines, drawing the scent into his mouth. Something about it…

—want—

He padded deeper into the forest on silent paws and broke into a run.

CHAPTER TWO

IF DEBAUCHERY WERE A COLOGNE, it would smell like the chapter house. Cloying high notes of sex and motor oil against a background of stale beer, tobacco, and rancid fryer grease. It permeated everything, floating with the dust through the shafts of weak sunlight, encrusting the couch cushions, and seeped into the roughly woven '80s plaid, aging it to a dingy gray-green muddle.

Kit put a shaking hand to the doorjamb, seeing the common room with its pool tables and long oaken bar through an overlay of the past. Her fingers swept over the wood-paneled wall riddled with gouges and scrapes, to the knothole packed tight with bubblegum.

She couldn't do this.

She closed her eyes and tried to regulate her breathing. To not think about being squished under that sofa, cat dander thick in her nose. The stench of tragedy dragged her back in time…

"Stop it!"

Flesh strikes flesh and her eyes screw shut. Knees to chest, she clenches her jaw, counting. Numbers were safe. Didn't change. One plus one was always—

Glass breaking. Her fists ball up, press to her temples.

"Goddamn it, Marie, you're mine!"

"Fuck you, Clay! We're leaving! I won't be part of your Goddamned harem! You're all animals!"

"And Reaper ain't? The fuck you say? Say it again. I fucking dare—"

A slap. "At least he just wants me! You're animals! Filthy—"

"He don't want you, he wants—"

A chair scraped across the floor, the sound rending through the memory. Kit fell back against the jamb, ready to bolt.

Nope. Couldn't do this.

Uneven footsteps. The door to the office at the far end of the room flew open and a man limped out with a cane, cellphone at his ear. Tall, wiry, with a salt-and-pepper ponytail and cheekbones sharp enough to cut, his eyes locked on hers, and he drew up short.

"Nix that, I got her." He ended the call and shoved the phone into his pocket.

He wasn't Claymore.

Kit's knees went weak, relieved and aching. She caught herself just before she slumped against the doorframe. *Fuck, get it together, girl! He's dead!* Shit, maybe she did need to see him in that box. Too late now. The man that'd come out of the office looked just as shaken, staring at her like he'd seen a ghost. Had he been there that night?

Whatever, didn't matter. She cleared her throat. "You Mud Knuckle?"

"MK, yeah... Kit Kat?"

No. She wasn't eight years old anymore. Her stomach roiled. *Come on, girl, time to channel some badass bitch.* "My name's Katherine."

"Ah. Right. Katherine." He wiped his palms down his shirt, looking around the empty room like someone was gonna appear and save him. "You make the service? Heard it was... nice. Flowers, casket... ol' ladies did it up right. Gonna be a potluck here after the ride, if you..."

She glared at him, and he had the decency to look abashed.

"So… you're here to stay."

"No. I'm here to ride out this shitstorm. Soon as it passes, I'm gone."

He scratched the back of his neck. "Yeah… about that…"

"Something you wanna tell me?"

"Ah, nah… just might take a spell." MK's gaze slid over her, a cunt-hair shy of leering. *Jesus, they're boobs, get over it. God, men sucked.* "Things is complicated."

Kit laughed. Story of her fucking life. "Un-complicate it and speak slow so my poor molly brain can comprehend." 'Cause that's all he saw her as, right? Some stupid shifter clubhouse slut.

"Kit Kat, it ain't—"

"My name is Katherine, and don't fucking tell me what it ain't. Look, you know what? Whatever, I don't give a fuck. Do whatever you gotta do to get me out of this shithole as soon as humanly possible. Which room is mine?"

"It ain't…"—He held his hands up at her glower—"Room ain't ready. Didn't know when you were comin' and what with the funeral—look, how about we talk some? Set you up some place in town." He pushed the open door behind him wide in invitation.

Kit's arms crossed over her stomach, trying not to hurl. "I'm not going in there."

MK winced. Guess he had been there that night, or at least seen the aftermath. "Right—"

His phone rang, and he snagged it, frowning at the screen. "Damn it…" he muttered, waving at the wall of booze behind the bar. "Get comfortable, I'll try and make this quick." By his tone, that wasn't gonna happen. He retreated into the office, slamming the door behind him.

Un-fucking-believable. Kit slumped against the wall, running a hand down her face. Leave. She should just leave…

Except there wasn't any place left for her to go. Not until MK set her up with that room, which she had to admit, sounded a hell of a lot better than bedding down here.

Her brow furrowed at the office door. Ten minutes. She'd give him ten minutes.

Ugh! How did she get herself into these situations? The one place she'd sworn up and down she'd never set foot in again, and boom, here she was.

She pulled out her phone and held it up, her boots crunching through peanut shells and worse as she walked around the room. Not a single damned bar. How did he have service? Fuck! If there ever was a time she needed Chanté's advice... Half a minute in, and the woman would be talking her through making Molotov cocktails so Kit could cross one of those "get closure," items off her bucket list. Hell, then she could backtrack with a bottle and go twerk on the asshole's grave.

Screw it. She'd start the party now.

Kit zipped up her hoodie and stomped behind the bar, unable to wrap her head around the fact Claymore'd actually been buried. She'd assumed he would've been cremated, you know, some bullshit biker freedom thing, not rotting in a box six feet under. Now where the hell was the... Heyyy... Hello, top-shelf tequila. Not about to shed a tear for cheating on her regular boy, José, she snagged the bottle, then a stool at the end of the bar, and plunked down with a sigh.

She shouldn't be surprised. The first eight years of her life had been straight-up lies. The night she'd seen her mother gunned down had made that abundantly clear. She wasn't Claymore's kid. She was a pawn he was holding against the fucking stalker psycho who was her real sperm donor.

Reaper. Name was even more fucked-up than Mud Knuckle.

And definitely more accurate.

Mama...

Kit wiped a finger beneath her eyes and picked at the bottle's label. At least Reaper didn't pretend to be something he wasn't. Nope. She'd never really known Claymore outside of his bullshit edicts on how she was supposed to live her life. Maybe someone hated him as much as she did and wanted his corpse to suffer. *How's it feel having someone lock you in a box, Claymore, baby? You feel safe?*

She smirked at the irony.

Whatever. It didn't matter. He didn't matter. No way was she trudging through some mucky cemetery to visit his bloating corpse. Forget her bestie's dubious assertion of how cathartic tossing a handful of dirt onto his grave and following it up with a hefty gob of spit would be. Even Chanté would pick saving a pair of shoes over some bullshit closure. Especially when they were vintage Doc Martens.

Okay, knock-off vintage Doc Martens, but who the hell in this hick town would know?

Fuck, their nasty shifter asses would probably smell the lie.

God, why did she care? Kit squeezed her eyes shut, her impending migraine threatening to go full-blown. Coming back upstate was a mistake. She could feel it, the ache in her bones as soon as she'd driven over the county line. The whole reason she'd let Claymore dictate her existence for so long.

She wouldn't become a monster like them. Wouldn't succumb to the animal.

That part of her didn't exist.

In the city it'd been easy to ignore, especially working three jobs to make rent and Taco Tuesday on the reg. That was her life. Her super exhausting, borderline comfortable, very safe life.

Until it wasn't anymore.

Fucking shifter assholes.

Whatever. Kit, no, *Katherine* Parson was too good for

Flatts, New York. She'd ride out this fucked-up psycho stalker bullshit, and then she was out.

Yeah. Keep telling yourself that.

Kit scrubbed at her face and checked the time. Five minutes already burned. Fuckity fuck fuck. In another hour and a half this place would be swamped with delusional, knuckle-dragging bikers coming to pay homage to their alpha. Kit supposed she had to give credit where credit was due. If nothing else, Claymore had been a charismatic leader.

Kind of like Napoleon, and she wasn't talking about Dynamite.

Fuck it. Chanté was always nagging her to celebrate the small stuff—She spun the cap off the bottle, planning on being holed up somewhere with the door barricaded long before anyone showed. In the meantime, Katherine, party of one, was drinking the good shit.

Hold up—that probably called for a glass, you know, to keep it classy. She leaned over the bar to grab one, ass in the air and laughed. Yeah, super classy, but whatev.

The man was dead, and she sure as hell could drink to that.

———

Grim stalked out of his room at the clubhouse, pulling on his spare cut and wincing. Jesus fuck, he needed a drink. Run hadn't done jack to mellow the beast, that weird scent was still stuck in his nose, and he was all keyed up over the steaming pile Stitch had dropped on him.

Didn't help that the motherfucker was right about getting his dick sucked. Grim would trade a bottle for a bj in a heartbeat, but when the fuck had his beast ever given a shit about what he wanted? He was lucky if the furry fucker let him get it up long enough to jack off.

[ANGER]

Yeah, yeah. He walked into the bar. *Save it for—*

Across the room, a perfectly heart-shaped ass offered itself up at eye-level.

"Goddamn…" Grim murmured, wiping a hand across his mouth, intent as its owner put a knee on the bar, rummaging behind it. Head down, ass up… He bit back a groan, taking in her parted thighs and the darker bit of fabric between them stretched taut enough to see the outline of plump lips.

Her hips canted, and his nostrils flared at the influx of her scent, his dick punching a tent in his jeans. *The fuck?* He grunted, adjusting himself. *Now?*

—want—

Grim couldn't argue. He moved closer as she slid back onto her stool, a familiar oversized hoodie hiding sinful curves.

His grin stretched to his ears.

Well, well, well. What were the Goddamned odds…

Not for the first time since he'd seen her sprinting away, he wondered who that damned sweatshirt belonged to. It was way too big to be hers. He wanted it gone, along with the fucker who gave it to her, and her all up in something of his.

Like his bed.

His cock kicked in agreement. Jesus fucking Christ, the woman was even more holy shit hot than he remembered. She tensed as he perched on the stool beside her, acting like he wasn't there and pouring herself three fingers.

"Tequila?" His voice came out in a rumble, his beast way too close to the surface.

—want—

She shivered like she knew it. Had she thought about him like he'd been thinking about her? Skating those long fingers between her legs the way he'd been stroking his cock? They tightened around her glass, and she raised it, shooting back its contents in one ill-advised mouthful. Grim frowned. Shit was gonna fuck her up—

Not even a grimace. Nice.

"It *was* tequila," she drawled, her warm tenor going straight to his dick.

"Mind if I join?"

She glanced over, then away, all dismissive.

Yeah, she remembered him. *Challenge accepted, baby.*

A scarf held back hair so dark it shone blue where the light hit it, and those almond eyes—Okay, those were pretty much telling him to fuck off, but he could smell the lie. She was into him. He grinned, fingering the memory of her fist hitting his jaw, and she flipped a long ebony lock over her shoulder.

—want—

Yes, we do... Damn, what the fuck did MK have the heat set at in here? Grim pushed up the sleeves of his Henley, and she snuck another peek at him. Her gaze trailed the tattoos spiraling from his knuckles to his forearms, then jumped to the ink at his open collar, following it up his throat—

Eyes whiskey-dark caught his, her pupils blowing wide just like that night. He palmed across the growing wet spot on his thigh, nostrils flaring at the punch of her arousal in the air. *Mmm. Yeah. That's what I'm talking about...* Grim stretched a leg behind her stool, juddering it closer.

"Hey! You mind?" She pulled away, wobbling. He shot out a hand to steady her, and she bit back a gasp at his touch. Fuck, she was just a little thing under that damned hoodie.

"Careful." He grinned, releasing her to pour another. "I'm Grim. Didn't expect you to follow me home. You stalking me, baby?"

Her eyes widened comically. "What? I—no... No! God, are you serious?" She shook her head, clearly flustered and pissed off about it, those lush lips of hers flattening to match her glare. "What kind of a name is Grim?"

A shitty one. He shrugged. "I'd ask my mama, but she's thirty-two years dead. And you are?"

Color bloomed over cheeks and she winced. "Kit—I mean, Katherine. And my stool was fine where it was."

Goddamn, she was fucking adorable on top of gorgeous. "Mmm. I like you close. Wouldn't want you to cut out on me again."

She snorted like she was daring him to stop her if she tried.

Oh baby, please try…

—chase—

Fuck yeah. Grim grinned, his fingers dropping from the edge of the bar to dust her thigh. He snagged her glass and took a sip. "If you're not stalking me, what do I owe this visit to, Kitten?"

"I thought I told you not to touch me," she grumbled, not pulling away. "And really, Kitten?"

The look on her face was priceless. He smirked at her indignation and licked along the glass's rim. Kit took a ragged breath and dropped her gaze, fisting her hands inside those massive sleeves and rubbing her thighs together.

—wants us—

Fuck yeah, she does. Were her nipples hard? The scent of her arousal was driving him and his cat crazy. So was being unable to see the rest of her. That damned hoodie needed to go. Grim set the glass down, fingers coasting to her inner thigh.

"Yeah, Kitten, cause this pussy's crying to be pet."

CHAPTER THREE

OHGODOHGODOHGOD…

Kit froze, totally blanking as Grim pivoted on the stool, his thighs caging hers. Shit. How was this player throwing her off her game? Yes, he was stupidly hot, but it's not like she'd never been hit on by a fuckboy before. Flirting was part of her damned job at Skin, and for Christ's sake, she was at the top of her class, telling them to piss off with a smile. As in zero tolerance, zero fucks given—

Grim moved closer, all six-plus gorgeous feet of him, fingers trailing a line of fire to the apex of her legs. She bit the inside of her cheek, nose twitching at the inrush of feline musk and man. Her eyelids fluttered. God, it was like some cracked-out combo of lemon spice, juniper, and drier sheets she just wanted to roll around in. To taste. To run her tongue along those tattoos spiraling up forearms the size of her calves. Damn, he probably had full sleeves…

His thumb brushed over her clit, and Kit bit back a groan, so wanting to give a fuck.

"Mmm… purr for me, Kitten…" He leaned in, thumb circling, nosing just below her ear, a deep rumble in his chest. Kit's palms slapped against it, fighting the urge to arch into him and bare her throat. Dayum… his pecs were *tight*… and sweet baby Jesus, he had a nipple ring.

What the hell, girl? Hello, number one rule, do *not* get

sucked in by the sexy. Her thighs parted. She knew better, but the vibe this dude was rockin'… she wanted more than a piece, she wanted the whole tie me-up-and-spank-me-daddy fantasy Chanté was so into.

His fingers swept the inner seam of her yoga pants and Kit's eyes fluttered closed, hips tilting. A needy sound that was *so* not her escaped her lips. All right, the fantasy less the daddy part, but—

"Fuck, you're wet… You gonna give me a taste of that cream?" His scruff scraped along her jaw, tongue lapping into the hollow below her ear…

Her eyes sprang open.

Hell no! Kit pushed him away, wiping away his spit with a sleeve. He frickin' chuckled like she was cute or some shit. Kitten. Where the hell did he get off? She'd make him fucking eat—

He sniffed his fingers, then sucked them off slow, his gray eyes smoldering.

Yeah… never mind what she wanted to make him eat.

No! Fuck no!

And a little bit yes…

Okay, more than a little.

Damn! What was she thinking? Fucking—shit, just kissing this man or any other shifter would bring her beast out of dormancy.

Saliva, blood, or semen. Any of theirs in her could trigger the first shift.

Not happening. Not now, not ever.

So why wasn't she beating feet?

Fuck. Was this some freaky shifter woo she didn't know about? Her pulse kicked up with a burst of anger. MK needed to hurry the fuck up.

"Ever heard of personal space?" She glared. "Stay out of mine."

Yup. She was just gonna play it off like none of that had

just happened.

Grim sat back and tucked a wave of wheaten hair behind his ear—also pierced—then scratched his jaw, manscaped scruff bristling loud in the silence between them. His lips twitched like he knew a secret, and Goddamn if she didn't want to throat punch him and kiss the shit out of him at the same time.

Pull it together, girl!

His tongue darted out to wet his bottom lip, teeth catching the enticing bit of flesh on its retreat. God frickin' damn. She snagged the bottle and tipped it back. Because that would solve all her problems.

Fuck classy.

Grim tsked and downed what was left in the glass. "I thought we were sharing."

His quicksilver gaze trapped hers, and he licked along the rim again. Kit coughed, choking on her mouthful with a sudden visual of exactly what that tongue could do, the aching burn in her throat echoing the one between her thighs. His nostrils flared, pupils expanding, then contracting into oblong slits, slapping her upside the head with what he was. A wicked grin played across his lips, and she wasn't havin' any of it.

Share? Like her father had shared his bed with every willing molly lifting their tails around the club? Fucking cats.

"I don't *share*," she snapped, raising the bottle again. Not her glass, not her personal space, and she sure as hell wouldn't be sharing his bed or whatever wall he thought he was going to throw her up against. Man was nothing but a fucking tom looking for some easy pussy, and she was not it.

He chuckled again, leaning back like he was taking her all in and knocked his knuckles against the bar. Stars were tattooed across his fingers. "That right?" His grin widened at her glare, flashing too-white teeth, his canines pointier than they had been.

Kit swallowed past the lump in her throat. Shit.

"Then answer the question, Kitten. Why are you here?"

———

—WANT—

Goddamn, this woman was killing him and his beast. Hot, cold, pissed off, and so fucking wet... She swiveled on her stool, smacking his leg away and turning back to the bar like she hadn't been ready to bend over for him two seconds ago.

She was fucking fascinating. Why wouldn't she tell him why she was here? Was she playing hard to get? No, this was a different game, a new game, and he and his beast were all in. He maneuvered his stool, edging behind her, and caging her against the bar.

"N-none of your business." She swallowed, trying to put distance between them again.

Wasn't happening.

Fuck, she made his tail twitch, and his hand ached to slap that ass. "Huh, and here I thought being VP meant everything in this club was my business." He brushed her thick silken locks aside to inhale along her nape, his dick throbbing for a real taste of her. Goddamn, he wanted to wrap her hair around his fist, push her against the bar—

She tensed, breath speeding with her pulse. His nose ghosted over it. Mmm. That elusive something mixed with citrus, cinnamon, and heat.

It was definitely her scent his cat had been following. Was she a half-breed? Not quite cat, but sure as hell didn't smell human, and that something... His canines extended, mouth filling with saliva, the urge to bite her intense.

—want—

The fuck is it about her?

—mate—

Grim snorted. *In your dreams, buddy.* His brow furrowed as

he nosed the divot below her ear. Definitely wasn't the scent of another shifter on her, the whisper of taste her lips had left on the glass and the musk on his fingers said she was unclaimed, but Jesus. If there was even a slim chance his cat was right, the idea of someone else—

—MINE!—

Grim's chest rumbled, cat's emotions bleeding into his. His hands tightened around her waist, the flare of her hips dimpling beneath his fingers so fucking sweetly. Anything with a dick needed to steer clear.

He rubbed his stubbled cheek against Kit's, releasing his pheromones and marking her as his, fingers drifting back between her thick thighs—

She jerked away like he'd burnt her. "Oh, no. Nope. I'm out. I'll find my own damned room. We're done here."

The acrid scent of her fear punched Grim in the gut, and he stumbled from his stool. She shot him double birds and was gone.

—?—

The fuck if I know… He wiped the back of his hand across his mouth, dick wilting despite his throbbing balls. Had he really read her that wrong? The way her car peeled out of the lot seemed to support the theory, but the damp patch on her stool told a different story.

"The hell was that?" MK stood in the office doorway with a manila envelope, watching her taillights wink out of sight. He turned to Grim, sniffing, then swore, pinching the smell from his nose.

He'd get over it.

"What was that? That was a fucking puzzle." Grim poured himself some more tequila, fingering the moist spot on the cushion beside him. Shifter or not, women knew coming here meant they were signing up to be a molly, which meant putting out for room and board. Her not wanting him had to have been an act. Even a half-breed molly—

—mate—

—or whatever the fuck she was, the mating pheromones she'd been putting out had been screaming for him to bend her over. Maybe she was in heat—No, that didn't make sense…

"You have any idea who that was?"

Grim glanced at the man and did a double take. Why the fuck did MK look pissed? It wasn't like he gave a shit about who fucked his other daughter. In fact, he'd all but delivered Nikki to Grim's door. Not that they'd been *fucking* fucking, but nobody was supposed to know about that.

He shrugged. "Another one of yours?"

MK frowned, snagging a bottle from the wall. "No. That was Marie's kid."

Grim jerked back like he'd been tased. What? "I thought she was dead."

Holy… Jesus fuck. That meant… maybe Satan's Vengeance hadn't been at the club for them that night. Kit's mom Marie had come into the picture several years after Reaper and Clay had fallen out over Grim's mother, and it'd been *déjà vu* all over again. Made no fucking sense, considering there wasn't exactly a shortage of female shifters and Marie was human, but whatever. Somewhere along the line, Reaper knocked Marie up despite her being Clay's ol' lady. Then a bunch of shit went down that resulted in Satan's Vengeance storming their MC, Reaper being incarcerated, Marie left in a vegetative state, and the kid dead.

Or so Grim'd been told.

"For all intents and purposes, she was," MK said. "Clay's been squirreling Kit away in the city since shit went down with her mama. About a month ago, one of Reaper's boys spotted her dancing at that club. Girl looks just like the woman. Reaper caught wind, and well, can't say I'm shocked at his reaction." MK shrugged, flipping over a glass to fill. "Man executed a full-frontal assault to get a hold of Kit back then. Who the fuck knows what he'd do now? Clay tried to explain shit and get her clear, but the speciesist fucks that raised her screwed that pooch. She weren't havin' none of it."

"You telling me she hates shifters?"

MK pursed his lips then shrugged, pouring himself a shot. "I'm telling you the only reason Ki—Katherine's—here is because Reaper's been playing one of his fucked-up cat and mouse games with her since he got out of the pen. Girl ain't got no place left to go. Clay must've offered her up sanctuary at some point, and she's scared enough to take it. His will's got it all in black-and-white." He tossed an envelope onto the bar and jerked his chin after it. "If you'd read the fucking thing, you'd know who he expected to babysit."

Grim stared at him, shit starting to make more sense than he was comfortable with… but offering the molly—

—our mate—

Keep telling yourself that.

—sanctuary was gonna start another war.

Shit, it already had, and Clay was the first casualty.

—kill Reaper—

Are you fucking serious? We had the chance at the club, and you turned tail!

[SHAME]

—different—

Riiight. I'm not signing up to get my ass beat again just to prove you're full of shit. Not that it wasn't fun, I mean, we haven't needed a breathing tube yet. Maybe we'll score one next time.

[ANGER]

Yeah, I can relate. Grim dragged a hand through his hair. All this shit over fucking mollys. He didn't get it. Why they had to get their dicks wet in the same damn hole not once, but twice… Fucking Clay. Didn't make sense. The man had been smarter than that, and Reaper… well, he was just batshit crazy. He'd put a fucking bullet in Marie's skull for raising Kit as Clay's, for Christ's sake.

Grim threw back his tequila, thumb rubbing over the glass as he swallowed, wishing it washed away the bitter taste in his mouth. Clay had raised Kit as his own. For eight Goddamned years while Grim, his actual fucking blood, had been—

Nope. Wasn't going there.

[SHAME]

What a clusterfuck. An inbred, backwoods, Goddamned *Springer Show* clusterfuck. "Kit's staying?" he asked, swiping up the envelope and folding it to jam into his jacket.

"Said something about 'until this shitstorm passes.' " MK shot him a look from beneath his brows and poured himself another. "Was gonna get her a room in town."

"Not here? How the fuck's that gonna work?" No way Reaper was gonna leave her alone now that he'd found her, and the man's attention wasn't fucking pleasant, regardless of kinship. "She doesn't have a clue how fucked she is, does she?"

"Nope," MK said, popping the P and ignoring Grim's initial question. "And if he don't know she's back in town already, her storming out of here like a bat out of hell is gonna clue him right in. Was hopin' to slip her in somewhere, but that ain't happenin'."

Grim grunted his agreement about Reaper knowing she was in town, not about slipping her in anywhere. That was just straight-up stupid, especially if the MC had a rat on Reaper's payroll. Their tech nerd seemed clean after some seriously strident questioning, but who the fuck knew? Grim was having a hard time trusting anyone.

Un-fucking believable, and the thought of what that piece of shit, Reaper, was capable of once he got his psycho paws on her—

[RAGE]

Grim's fingernails elongated, scoring the bar top as his hand fisted.

Fuck, yes, I get it! He pushed his beast back down. "I need you to put eyes on her until this circle jerk for Clay's done with. Mike and Pete still at the gate?"

MK snorted. "You really want those two fucktards tailing her?"

"Unless you're volunteering, everyone else is gonna be at the ride, and it's not like they're particularly effective sentries."

"Point taken." MK scowled, rubbing at his leg. Witches had set it to rights, but in this weather, it had to be aching something fierce. "I'll send 'em out."

"Any idea where she would've gone?" Town wasn't huge, but it drew tourists from the city like flies on shit this time of year. Had to be three dozen places scattered about the mountain where she could hole up.

MK threw back his shot and hissed air in through his teeth. "House's probably a safe bet."

That dump? Place was a fucking hovel. Power had been cut years ago after a tree ripped through the lines and punched a hole in the roof. Clay'd had it fenced off as a hazard, but that hadn't deterred the kids in town from claiming it to party and fuck in. Christ, she was going there?

"The hell is she thinking?"

MK shook his head, anger back in his eyes. "Could ask you the same. Not a chance that girl's first shift's been triggered, and your dumb ass went and marked her. Probably scared the shit out of her with way she's been raised… ain't no way she's down to change."

Grim felt himself pale. Saliva, blood, or semen. Shit, no wonder she'd freaked and wouldn't share a glass with him after he'd licked the damned thing. He dropped onto a stool and dragged over the bottle of tequila. Well, that piece of the puzzle fit. She was so damned contradictory because her body wanted what her mind sure as hell didn't.

He could fucking relate and would back off. Nobody

deserved having their biology used against them. Damn, did she even know what kind of signals her cat was putting out? If she'd never shifted, that wasn't outside the realm of possibility…

—*want!*—

Yeah, but she doesn't. Not the two-legged side of her at least. Grim sighed, rubbing at the abrupt ache in his chest. "She's an unaffiliated female in my territory. You know how that works."

"Ain't your territory yet." MK threw back his shot and ran his tongue over his teeth. "And I damned well do know how it works. That weren't approval for her to raise her tail around the club you rubbed up on her, it was for everyone else to back the fuck off. You tryin' to yourself lynched? 'Cause I'm pretty sure I know who'll lead the mob."

Shit. Nikki.

—*cum-slut*—

The claws were back.

Fuck her. As in seriously. Fuck her and fuck everything she had on him. Bitch was far from lily white, and Stitch was right. The shit she was pulling had to stop.

[ELATION]

"Just like your Goddamned daddy," MK growled, eying the fresh gouges in the wood. "You bite yourself a queen, and you still just gotta stick your dick in every cunt—"

Grim shot to his feet with a growl, looming over the shorter man. "Shut your fucking mouth."

MK stumbled back against the wall of booze, sending bottles clanking, the power in Grim's voice shocking the shit out of them both.

Holy fuck, had he just—His mouth went dry. *This is the hill you're gonna die on? You seriously just issued a fucking alpha command over a molly we spent point three seconds with?*

[SMUG]

—*respect our mate*—

Respect. Right, except she's not.

—will be—

No, she—Christ, he wasn't getting into this with his cat. Asshole was unreasonable when he fixated on something. Wait. Had he actually *fixated* on her? Like, true mate-type shit?

Fucker was suspiciously silent, and Grim groaned.

Tell me I'm wrong and this isn't like that cattail you swore was a squirrel.

Silence.

Goddamn it, he didn't have time for this shit. It was bad enough there was no reset button on the furry fucker throwing down the gauntlet by issuing MK an alpha command, leaving Grim to deal with the consequences. He raked his hair back, Stitch's words from the cemetery pounding through his head.

… You're as alpha as Clay was. Time to own it…

Now he didn't have a fucking choice.

Grim laughed, pouring another glass. Fuck it. If his cat wanted to blow shit up, so would he. Grim toasted MK, threw back his shot, then cracked the glass onto the bar.

"Nikki's not a fucking queen, and that's not my bite. Bitch is just a molly like every other club whore lifting their tails around here."

"Ain't what she said."

Grim's eyes caught his. "She lied."

MK's gaze dropped to the floor, submissive. Grim grunted and looked away. The silence between them stretched, then the older man winced, pushing off the wall to stand.

"We done here?"

"Yeah, and I suggest you pass on the message. That shit she pulled with Miser's ol' lady was over the line and lying about having my bite's just digging her deeper. One more strike, and her exile's going up for a vote during church. Kit's got nothing to do with it."

"Keep tellin' yourself that," MK muttered, pouring himself another and looking at Grim askance. The lip of the bottle trembled against his glass.

Yeah, that's right. I just made you my bitch. "I'm telling you, and anyone else that gets in my face about it."

"Wasn't in your face, just…" MK dragged a hand down his long jaw. "Look, Nikki's on her way back with the rest of them mollys to set up for the potluck. Lemme talk to her. Meanwhile, you best get gone before she smells that girl on you."

Grim's eyebrow rose at MK's one-eighty.

The man's lips curdled, but he didn't meet Grim's eyes. "If you're finally manning up and claimin' alpha, I ain't gonna fight you on it. My job's to follow orders, and it's what Clay wanted," he grumbled, shaking his head. "Go on, keys to his bike are in the drawer where he left 'em. I'll get Mike and Pete on your girl."

Grim opened his mouth to argue the last point, and headlights washed across the back wall. Shit. That'd be Nikki with the rest of them. He grunted his thanks to MK and snagged the Indian's keys from the desk.

It was time to ride.

CHAPTER FOUR

KIT CLUNKED the car door shut and leaned against it, mouth agape.

You gotta be shitting me.

The farmhouse where she'd spent the first eight years of her life was trashed and in the middle of a puddle the size of Grand Central. As in, not fucking approachable by car, or habitable in general.

She choked back a sad laugh. So much for staying here until she got her shit together. The front porch sagged in places like it was wheelchair accessible, all the windows were busted out, and a damn tree had caved in half the roof.

Her fingers laced through the rusted, vine-choked chain-link surrounding the field the house was swimming in, her eyes brimming. *Get it together, girl. You had a plan.*

Yeah. About that…

Whelp, she could skip line item 1, "Moving in," and head on over to line item 2, which basically consisted of, "What the fuck am I gonna do now?"

Crickets.

Next was seeing if anyone in town was hiring, but that would have to wait until Monday. Between the funeral today, and a full day of Bible-thumping tomorrow, nothing was gonna be open. Which left her plenty of time to obsess over Grim.

Ugh! The one man she'd ever crushed on, and he's a damned shifter. Just thinking about that smile of his, the way his left cheek creased into one long dimple... His thumb circling her clit.

God*damn*, no man should be able to use his thumb like that. Her thighs squeezed together, and she swore, snatching her drifting hand back.

No! Nope. I am not gonna go there—

—You mean again? Girl, please. You're crushin' on the man hard. Don't even play like you haven't been fingering yourself on the reg since you saw that big, beautiful, blinged-out dick pissing in the sink...

Oh, sweet baby Jesus, that piercing through his crown...

Well, now that one part of her was uncomfortably warm— Ugh, stop it!

Had to be shifter woo. *Get it together, Kit, it's all just some mind fuck...*

She tucked her traitorous hands into her sleeves, breath frosting from her lips. Monday. Think about Monday. She'd hit the diner first. A week or two of tips would get her to Ottawa with enough to pay for a room, and that's a wrap. No more hot shifter temptation. And since Reaper was a felon, they wouldn't let him across the border, right?

Riiight.

The wind kicked up, and the scarf in her hair went flying before she could free her numb fingers from her sleeves. Oh, no, no, no! Chanté had given her that for luck—

God, it was a sign.

Kit laughed, watching it disappear into the waterlogged bracken across the field.

Luck had literally just deserted her.

The steady mist plaguing the mountains all day turned to a hard drizzle. Yeah, the universe was definitely telling her it was time to shit or get off the pot. She wrapped her arms around herself, shivering. Her hoodie was no match for

October in the Adirondacks. She sighed, not about to kid herself that there was something warmer in the house she could snag.

Her vision blurred. She plopped back into the front seat of her hatchback and sniffed... As much as she didn't want to, she'd be stupid not to case the place.

Bright side, Kit. Find the bright side.

And there were those damned crickets again.

Maybe there was something inside she could pawn?

Right. So go check it out.

She met her own eyes in the rearview. "You got this. Now dig out those ugly-ass boots from the back and hop to."

It was stupid, but just thinking about the tacky-as-sin rhinestone rain boots made her feel better. Chanté had been trying to pawn them off on her since the first and last secret Santa they'd done three years ago, and it'd been a hard no. Kit never thought she'd be grateful ending up with the bedazzled size thirteens.

Not that she'd ever tell Chanté, but considering that morass around the house had to be a good six inches deep... She dug them out of the back and jammed her feet in. Damn, they were ugly. She laughed, blew out a breath, and winked at herself in the rearview mirror.

"You got this."

Her reflection didn't look so sure. Whatever, fuck that bitch. Even if she didn't have it, she sure as hell could fake it and would be damned before any of those shifter assholes saw her sweat.

She lost a boot twice to the sucking mire before she made it onto the front porch. The boards sagged beneath her feet like wet noodles. God, this place hadn't aged well, and it was even more of a shithole up close.

She fought to turn the knob, shouldering the door to—it gave abruptly, and she barely caught herself from sprawling over the worn, wooden floor. Her fingers scraped over the wall and flicked the switch.

Nothing. Because of course. Had she seriously expected it to work?

Maybe…

Kit swore at herself, kicking through drifts of beer cans, cigarette butts, and condom wrappers on her way to the kitchen. Back door had blown open and a shattered bulb hung over a crappy Formica table. Her breath clouded around her. She slammed the door shut and clomped over to the stove to spin a dial. Nope. Gas was dead, too. Sighing, she leaned over the sink, looking out the grayed window.

Backyard had been eaten by the surrounding woods, a rusted swing set peeking from a curtain of yellowed bittersweet and briars. She pulled out her phone, hand trembling.

Still no service.

Her fingers swiped over the table, leaving long pale streaks. Years of filth coated every surface, and nothing came out of the tap when she turned it on. There was probably an ocean of funk in the basement from the pipes bursting. She scrubbed her hand against her pants, stubborn brown circles staining her fingertips.

Cupboards were empty save for a handful of bloated canned goods with gooey, blackened labels. Mice had long since made off with the paper goods and ruined the few linens crumpled against sagging baseboard heaters.

Kit ghosted through the downstairs. Kitchen, half bath, back bedroom. That was empty, save for a smattering of used condoms and a mattress that reeked like piss. In the living room, a lone loveseat vomited springs and stuffing, the walls tagged with lurid green dicks and redneck gang signs.

Nothing else was left. She wasn't sure what she'd expected… but it wasn't this. She wanted something. Something that proved she'd lived here. That a family had lived here. Some clue that at one point they'd been happy…

They had, hadn't they? The memories she had of her mom making pierogi… showing her how to crimp the edges. Claymore on that big bike with the ridiculous baby blue and yellow paint job she'd picked out… that was real, wasn't it?

Her fists bit into her temples, and she slumped against a wall, fighting tears. *Stop. It doesn't matter. You knew it was all lies —*

Then why did it hurt so bad?

She needed to do what she'd come to do and get the fuck out of there.

The stairs to the second floor loomed before her. Couldn't be any worse right?

It was worse.

The ceiling in the corner of the master bedroom had given away, churning gray sky visible through the hole. The walls sagged with water damage, swaths of black mold swirling over them in ribbons of decay. The bed frame barren and broken, listing to one side. Dressers entombed beneath moldering plaster and bird shit, drawers scattered or hanging askew. A bit of faded liner was still pinned inside the corner of one, red floral print faded to pink.

Kit crouched down and picked it out reverently… a vague memory of her mama laughing and a cloud of rose-scented talcum powder clouding the room… she held the scrap in her palm, stained fingers lightly dusting its surface. Humming a melody she'd forgotten.

She stood, her feet taking her past the full bath, eyes still on the fragile bit of her past. A crumbling bit of truth.

She stopped before the closed door at the end of the hall, carefully pocketing her prize, hand trembling on the knob to what had been her bedroom.

————

Grim sat on the roof of the clubhouse, propped up between the A/C handlers, nursing a bottle and freezing his balls off.

At least he had been. Now he was pretty fucking numb. Well, physically thanks to the Vicodin he'd popped. The ride through town had been a painful blur. He vaguely recalled saying something to the assembled brothers, but he'd be damned if he could remember a word of it. Probably better that way. He was shit at public speaking.

Down below, the party was in full swing and had been since the ride. He had zero interest, still tossing around the bomb MK'd dropped about Kit.

—want—

Mmm. Ditto, but we've been over this.

—wrong—

The furry fuck could suck it. *No, making her do shit she doesn't want to do is wrong.*

—wants us—

Like we wanted all those mollys?

[ANGER]

—different—

Same.

[FRUSTRATION]

Suck it up.

He wasn't touching her, as much as his dick ached to. And as for the impending fuckery Clay had initiated by offering her sanctuary… Shit.

Grim swished around a mouthful of booze. To be fair, the fuckery had been initiated thirty-two years ago and went by the name of Abigail. Or so he'd heard. Aside from the sainthood Reaper ascribed to her and whoredom the brothers downstairs slapped onto her memory, Grim didn't know much about his ma.

And Clay'd been silent on the subject.

The alpha had been a man of few words, his actions had spoken more than his mouth. Like when he showed up and hauled Grim out of Reaper's cellar by his scruff. Called him son and beat the fuck out of anyone who challenged him on it.

Taught him how to function on two legs. To be a man.

Eighteen years too late.

Shit. Grim scrubbed at his face, trying to forget everything that'd come before he'd been saved. Wondering for the millionth time why Clay hadn't claimed him as soon as he'd heard Abigail died whelping. Or when it became obvious Grim's sire was different from Grapple and Shiv's.

Now he'd never know.

Grim held the bottle up to the light. Should've brought up two. He wasn't nearly drunk enough to be thinking about that shit. Not that the rest of the clusterfuck he was currently embroiled in was any better. He pinched a hand across his temples. Challenging for alpha. What the fuck had his dipshit cat been thinking?

...Time to own it... And that means coming clean, about all of it...

All of it. Fucking Stitch. Grim snorted, his cat suspiciously silent. Furry asshole would be. *Didn't think about that when you were slapping down that command, did ya? You ready to spill to everyone about being the star tom knocking up mollys in Reaper's side business, or just how he kept you so fucking feral with silver I couldn't shift back to two legs?*

—kill him—

Grim snorted, booze burning his sinuses. *That's the dream.* He sighed, watching the clouds swirl above. Storm was brewing, air tinged with snow.

And now that sadistic prick wanted Kit. Had to be for her genetics, since Marie had been human, they made Kit one hell of a prize. Reaper would be obsessed. It was rare for a human to get knocked up by a shifter, but when they did, any offspring was a coveted infusion of new blood to the paranormal community.

—No! Ours—

*Yeah, our—No! Fuck, get it through your—*Grim paused, ears pricking. Someone was coming up the fire escape. His gaze snapped to it, a low growl escaping his throat.

—cum-slut—

"So this is where you're hiding." Nikki's voice purred over the rooftop, all saccharine sweet and bitter at the same fucking time.

His teeth clenched. Goddamn it, he wasn't in the mood. She pulled herself up over the parapet and sauntered over. How she'd climbed up here in six-inch heels…

Grim turned away, his fist clenching the bottle's neck.

She stood over his outstretched legs, a stiletto to each side, and cleared her throat, pausing to make sure he checked out her pin-up perfect body. She smirked at the flick of his eyes, twirling a long lock of golden hair around a finger. He had to hand it to her, woman knew how to work those fake tits and thick thighs to compensate for her shitty personality. Half the club was waiting in line to lick her ass even after all the shit she'd pulled.

Not that his cock had ever twitched.

[SMUG]

"You need to leave."

Nikki laughed and leaned back against the A/C handler, spreading her long, toned legs. She lifted her flirty little skirt enough to drag a finger through her slit. "No, I need to come, and it's cold out here. You better hurry."

[DISGUST]

Grim took a long swallow from his bottle, wondering how drunk she was. "Go find someone actually interested."

"Awww, Grimmers, come on. You know I like the way you eat pussy best," she pouted, her eyes glinting. "And as your queen, I deserve the best. It's been too long since people have scented you on me. It's not healthy the way you're keeping to yourself so much. You don't want everyone thinking you're going feral again, do you?"

A growl crept up his throat. Goddamned manipulative— "You're not my queen yet, and why the fuck would they think that?"

"You've just been so distant." Nikki shrugged, all wide-eyed and totally full of shit. "Everyone's worried that this business with Clay might push you over the edge..."

She said it like the last time his cat had taken over and run amok hadn't been her fault.

And just like that, all the side-eye Grim'd gotten at the cemetery made a hell of a lot more sense. Bitch was chumming the water with his reputation, again.

[RAGE]

"And how'll that work out for your plans to become queen?" he spat.

"Mmm." She pouted, inspecting her manicure. "Daddy said something about us not being on the same page anymore. I'll admit you and I have had some issues, but thought we'd come to an understanding."

Grim growled. "An understanding? After you fucked the entire club behind my back, lied about having my bite, and keep pissing off the ol' ladies?"

"Oops." She shrugged like it was no big. "Guess you better hurry up and claim me as your queen. I'd hate to think you were reneging on our deal to make me the MC's alpha female. What would people say if they knew what you were doing in Reaper's cellar? All those poor mollys you barbed—"

"It wasn't like that and you know it," he ground out, more of a fucking victim than any of them had been. Reaper had made a Goddamned mint off pimping out his cat.

"Wasn't it, Grimmers? I know what story I'll tell. And all that guilt... It's no wonder you can't get it up for me. Honestly, if you got put down, it'd open up my options. I really am doing you a favor." She tongued a canine, her hand dropping to strum across her swollen cunt. The tang of her pheromones in the air proof positive she was getting off on threatening him.

Grim snorted. "A favor."

"Yeah, I mean, you're cute, but I'm beginning to think you're not worth the trouble." Her gaze hardened, and she jabbed a pointed heel onto his shoulder. "Change my mind."

His lip arched into a snarl.

—KILL—

Don't tempt me.

"Fuck off." He swept her foot away, wishing he could tear out her fucking throat without getting lynched. "Dirt hasn't even settled on Clay's grave. Show some fucking respect."

Nikki laughed, crossing her arms under her tits and plumping them up. "I'll never understand why you cared so much about a man who abandoned you—"

Grim was in her face, his hand around her throat, choking off her next words. She scrabbled at his wrist on tiptoe. "Shut. The fuck. Up."

A purr rumbled beneath his palm and her pupils dilated, the scent of her arousal cloying. Her core rubbed against his thigh. "Oh God, yes. Make me sorry, Grim," she gasped out.

He snorted, his lips brushing hers. "I'm sorry enough for the both of us." His teeth sank into her bottom lip, and she groaned, her fake tits straining against him. "Such a needy little whore. Damn, you're pathetic."

"Yes..." She fisted his shirt, chasing his lips as he pulled away and squealing at the cruel pinch to her nipple. "Oh, yes..."

He caught her jaw, fingers digging into her cheeks and meeting her lust-crazed gaze. Cunt had to be in heat. "Does it hurt, cum-slut? You want it that bad?"

"Oh God, so bad..."

"Get yourself started," he breathed, and her head tipped

back with a moan. She dropped a hand from his shirt, fingers plunging into her dirty hole. "That's it, work that cunt…" Grim stepped close, pressing her against the air handler.

Her leg rose to hook around his hip, and he batted it away. "Please, Grim…" she whined.

His nose skated over her throat, the scent of her healing bite turning his stomach.

"Harder, Nikki. Fuck yourself like you want me to."

She whimpered, and her hips jerked to obey.

"You thinking about how my cock would feel?" He pinched her tit, and she cried out. "How fucking hard I'd rail that sloppy slit of yours? What my cum would feel like smeared between your thighs?"

"Oh God, yes, I'm so—"

"Too fucking bad." Nikki's eyes widened as Grim dropped her, stepping back.

—laughter—

She cried out, knees hitting the roof hard and skittering peastone gravel. He crouched, brushing a brittle blonde lock from her face. "Go downstairs and service a brother, molly. Our deal is off. You'll never be a queen, mine or otherwise. And if you wanna hear a story, I'll tell the one about what went down at the last MC you were at. That'll go over with the brothers like a shiv during bed check. Walk the fuck away." He turned to leave.

"You're such an asshole!" She pushed up to sit, seething. "That's not how this works!"

"Nothing about us works. We're done." He snatched up his bottle and killed it, trying to wash the taste of her from his mouth.

[JOY]

She sat back on her haunches, a sly smile tilting her lips. Big blue eyes of malice glittered up at him through her fall of bleach-blonde hair. How someone so beautiful was so Goddamned rotten never ceased to amaze him. She flicked a lock behind her shoulder, running her fingers over the livid bite spanning her creamy white flesh.

"What's the matter? You jealous?"

He laughed, walking backward from her. "Jealous? Why the fuck would I be jealous? I feel sorry for the dumb fuck. You're a club whore, Nikki. A common molly. I don't give two shits who you service. It's your fucking job. Go do it."

—laughter—

The rage on her face put a huge grin on his. He winged his empty over the roof's edge, feeling lighter for the first time in forever.

Her gaze narrowed. "You're going to regret this, Grim."

Too late. I've regretted you for years... "Whatever you gotta tell yourself," he said, flipped a leg over the parapet and grinning again at her screech of frustration.

Stitch was waiting at the bottom of the ladder. He squinted up at the roof. "Guess Nikki found you. Do I wanna know?"

"I cut her loose."

Stitch's eyebrows shot up off his head. "And I thought after hearin' you smacked down MK with an alpha command, my day couldn't get any better." The old man beamed, slapping Grim's shoulder. "It's about fucking time. Doc can't stand her." He rubbed his hands together. "Bet she'll make a roast to celebrate."

Grim snorted. "Doc hates everyone."

"Nah... well, yeah, but this was a special kind o' hate."

"Whatever, if she's cooking, I'm there." Stitch's on-again-currently-off-again ol' lady didn't play in the kitchen; she owned it and everything else like a boss. "Any reason you're out here waiting for me?"

"Maybe nothin', maybe somethin'." Stitch shrugged, fiddling with his vape. "Them two idjits MK sent out to watch your girl ain't checked in for the past few hours. Last place they did was at Clay's old place."

—see, our girl—

"She's not mine," Grim muttered, a sour burn in his gut. "I'll check it out. Keep your phone close."

Stitch grunted, fishing into his pocket, then dangling keys. "Take my cage. Roads is icin' up fast and if somethin' happened, you ain't gettin' bodies out on the back of a bike."

"You think there's gonna be bodies?" he asked, palming them.

"Dunno, but if Reaper's involved, it ain't outside the realm of possibilities."

Grim swore. It was more than possible. Shit was inevitable.

CHAPTER FIVE

KIT'S BEDROOM door swung open, and she bit back a scream, falling back into the hall and hitting the floor hard. She scrambled to her feet, whimpering as Chanté's rain boots tripped her up.

He was here.

Her father. Sitting on the bare mattress in her old bedroom like he'd been waiting for her. Shit, had he been waiting for her? Why the fuck had she come?! A mistake, this was all one big fucking—

She had to get away.

Kit turned to sprint, and a frickin' behemoth came out of the bathroom, his thick arms surging around her, pinning her back to his chest. A brand of a crescent moon inside a pentagram flexed on his forearm. The shifters following her back in the city'd had those too, the same as from that night her mother…

Kit screamed, thrashing against him. He grunted, tightening his hold.

"Let go, you fucker!" She writhed, kicking and struggling and—

Snick snack.

—froze at the cold press of a racked gun against her temple.

"That's just about enough of that, darlin'." Reaper

grinned, a manic glint in his icy blue stare. The lines of his face were deeper, but, oh God… it was really him.

Her father.

Kit's heart thudded in her ears, sweat pricking her eyes. There wasn't—wasn't enough air—

He tsked, the gun's barrel smoothing the hair from her brow. "Mmm. Turned out just as feisty as your mama, now ain't ya?" Her gaze flicked back to his in surprise and he grinned. "Before she were ruined, that is. Not much of a fight in her these days… though I aim on tryin'."

He wetted his lips and grabbed his crotch.

Rage spiked through Kit. "Haven't you done enough to her?!"

… Mama was on the floor, dress torn and hiked up around her hips. Why didn't she move? Kit crawled from under the desk toward her, hands sticky and red… the blood… so much blood…

Kit's vision grayed, and he slapped her, bringing her back.

"I ain't done not nearly enough, and if you ain't just her spittin' image. Whoo! We got us another hellcat, Grapple!"

She screamed again, thrashing, and Reaper laughed.

"Yeah, we're gonna get on just fine… so as long as you learn to mind. I got plans for you, darlin', and I gotta say, when you lit out of the city, I did not figure on you deliv-erin' yourself here. Tell me true—you miss your sweet daddy?"

Kit bucked against the behemoth. "Fuck you, asshole!"

His grin got wider. "Now, I ain't that inbred, but Grapple here's itchin' to claim hisself a girl like you. Ain't that right, boy?" A hand with fingers like ham hocks pawed at her breast, and her eyes widened at the realization of what was jabbing into her spine.

"Mmm-hmm, seems he done approve. Shame he's already bitten off more'n he can chew—" Reaper sniffed, eyes narrowing. His frosty gaze skated over her, going colder. He pressed the gun up under her jaw, forcing her head back, then skated his nose along her throat, inhaling. "Well, I'll be... You been liftin' your tail for my nephew?"

His nephew? Who the hell was his—Her eyes went big. Wait, was Grim seriously—

THWACK.

Kit gasped, stars exploding across her vision at Reaper's backhand. That motherfucker had hit her.

He. Hit. Her.

A growl rippled from her father's throat, and she squeezed her thighs together to keep from pissing herself. She blinked back tears, watching the obscene slide of his finger stroking the gun's trigger. "Dirty, dirty girl. And here I thought you was keepin' yourself pristine..."

Kit's ragged breathing grew louder. Was he kidding?

Reaper's head abruptly cocked, a smile slicing ear to ear. He leaned back, all Mr. Congeniality, a thousand times more terrifying than before. "But then, my mama always said to take that skunk and make it a pie." He glanced over Kit's head at Grapple with a manic grin.

"What d'you say, boy? You got a hankerin' for somewhat?"

Grapple grunted, the thrust of his hips against her back leaving no doubt what his hankering was for.

"You're right, you're right..." Reaper mused, like they'd just had an enlightening discussion. He pulled at his gray-streaked goatee. "Catnip's just the thing, but Lord knows I ain't a patient man. What d'you say we speed destiny up a tick?"

Reaper's eyes flicked to Grapple, and the arms around her tightened, squeezing the breath from her. She opened her mouth, gasping. Reaper pinched her jaw wide—

Hawked, and spat into her mouth.

The gelatinous glob hit the back of her throat and Kit gagged. He slapped a hand over her face, pinching her nose shut before she could puke.

"There we go, darlin'," he crooned into her ear, trailing the gun's barrel up and down her throat. "Swallow like a good little whore for Daddy."

Her mind stuttered. She couldn't breathe—couldn't—didn't—

Her throat spasmed.

Oh, God.

"Good girl," he purred, nodding to Grapple.

The behemoth dropped her, and she fell, vomit spattering the floor before she hit, sour sick thick in her nose. Hot tears scoured her face, her insides twisting. Another greasy slick erupted from her lips, the stinking dregs of her humanity splattered and steaming in the dying light.

"Why are you doing this to me?" she whispered, her fingers fluttering against her swollen cheek, stomach cramping to rebel again. She'd shift, his spit was going to make her shift…

Reaper paused at the head of the stairs, his head cocked. " 'Cause the scripture done say 'tis a man's responsibility to do right by his kin. You tell your boyfriend that, Princess, and I'll be seeing you both real soon. Grapple, leave our boy an invite for the party he ain't gonna turn down."

A zipper hissed and a wet, stinking stream hit Kit's back. She sobbed, curling into a ball.

"Whoo, that's ripe!" Reaper cackled, waving a hand. "Eye-for-an-eye gets all them juices flowin', now don't it, boy?"

Grapple growled, pushing past him.

"You'd be right about that, and hot damn, if I ain't just got chills." Reaper's smile sliced across his face again and then he ambled down the steps after the behemoth, whistling.

———

Grim pulled the truck onto the trail head down the road from the house and slammed it into park, checking his cell again.

Those two dipshits still weren't answering their phones. Stitch was right.

Could be them being fucktards.

Could be a big fucking problem.

Grim eyed the setting sun through the arching skeletal branches above, ruddy behind the clouds. His money was on a problem. They were fucking stupid, but they were legacy and knew how this shit worked. If MK had told them to stake out the house, they'd stake out the house. Especially after fucking up and being pulled off gate duty.

So why weren't they checking in?

[UNEASE]

Grim slid from the cage, boots crunching through the iced-over mud, and headed through the woods.

He scratched his jaw as he picked his way through the forest, straining to hear anything over the wind and pinging fall of sleet on leaves. The trees held the dead silence of fear like a blanket tight to its chin.

—wrong—

Agreed. Something about this shit was definitely not right.

The faint whiff of teen boys and Kit's scent tickled his nose as he came to the fence enclosing the yard. He padded to a break in the chain-link, just another shadow in the deepening twilight.

Something fluttered in the bracken.

Grim knelt, pulling it free and holding it to his nose. His fingers tingled. It was Kit's scarf. The one that'd held back her hair at the bar, dark blue with tiny—he squinted at the pattern. Were those dicks?

—laughter—

Motherfucker. They were definitely dicks.

Snorting, he shoved it into his heavy leather jacket, looking across the overgrown yard. The glint of a bumper caught his eye. Her hatchback was in the drive.

He sat back on his haunches and glanced at his phone

again. Still nothing from Mike and Pete, and if they were still here, their teenaged funk should be a hell of a lot stronger. Had MK sent them somewhere else?

Fuck, maybe he had. No telling where the man's head was after Grim had smacked him down with that shit about his precious snake of a girl at the bar. Alpha command or no, Grim still wasn't technically the MC's prez, and if he had to finger a rat, MK was currently at the top of his vermin list.

He scrubbed at his face. But MK and Clay had been tight…

Or had been, until Nikki showed up, and the alpha had kicked her out of his bed with a heavy dose of humiliation. Grim frowned. Which was not so coincidently right before she'd cozied up to him. Shit. His theory she was the one feeding Reaper intel was becoming more credible. That dig about him being dead opening up other options…

Grim shook his head, skirting the fence's perimeter to the car. No. Nikki was a vindictive cunt, but she wasn't stupid. He still couldn't believe she'd throw in with Reaper, and options had nothing to do with it. He was too unpredictable for her to manipulate. She'd never give up that kind of power.

A man's waterlogged footprints led from the driver's side of Kit's car into the swamp surrounding the house.

The hell was that about? He growled. Only one way to find out.

Fucking water was so cold the top layer of rime splintered around his boots. He slogged through it, leaving a drunken line of sludge behind him. The rest of the frosted swamp looked untouched, and the house was dark, windows black voids swallowing the light.

A shiver ran up his spine that had nothing to do with the temperature. The porch groaned beneath his weight, a board giving and plunging his foot ankle deep into something disturbingly warm.

The scent of offal and teenaged boy wafted from the jagged hole.

Grim jumped back, landing on his ass in the mire, nasty water wicking through his clothes. He swore, breath coming fast, eyes on the pale flesh of a hand floating just beside the submerged steps.

Motherfucker. He pulled his cell, dialing as he stood.

Stitch answered on the third ring, breathing heavy. "This better be good."

"It ain't. You were right. There's a body at the house."

"Off." Sounds of a molly protesting and the rustle of cloth. "One of ours?"

"Yeah."

A belt buckle clanked, and a door slammed open. Music blared. "Who?"

"Can't tell."

Stitch swore. "Leaving now."

The phone cut out and Grim tucked his away, trading it for his piece. He racked it, giving the hole a wide berth and pushing the front door open. It gave a Godawful screech. Slowly, he stepped inside—

[RAGE RAGE RAGE]

Grim crumpled under his cat's assault for control, fur sprouting and nails elongating as he gagged on the sour musk of piss marking the house as another male's territory.

Fuck. Not just any male's… Grapple's. What the fuck did his brother—

—MINE!—

He fell to his knees, fighting the twist and crack of his spine reforming. His gun clattered across the floor.

Beast was going feral.

Not again, not now—

Back the fuck off!

—No!—

Yes, you dumb fuck! Grim's clawed hand raked long gouges

across the floor, panting. *Think, asshole! You come up on her like this, and she'll lose her shit! Let me do this!*

—…—

His body froze, mid shift, and the cat retreated. Grim reversed the change, groaning as he reassumed his human form. Aching and bathed in cold sweat, he stood bent over, hands on his knees, ribs killing him. Jesus fuck, that'd been close.

—seething—

He swept his gun up off the floor. *It's called impulse control, asshole! Work on it.*

His cat chuffed, hackles still raised. Grim frowned at the distinct sense of, "sorry not sorry" the furry fuck was putting off, and pinched at his nose, taking stock. Place was fucking rank. Beneath the piss, the smell of vomit and the coppery tang of a fresh kill hung heavy in the air, along with a delicate thread of citrus and cinnamon.

Kit.

Three of those things came from upstairs, and as for the fourth… he had a feeling whichever of the boys he was picking up on was beyond his help.

He stared up into the darkness of the stairwell and eased up the edges of the treads, wincing as they protested his weight. Didn't give a shit about the noise. If Reaper and his shithead brother were still here, they would've jumped him when he was fighting with his cat. Falling through the damned things was another matter.

Praying the steps held, he continued up, the stench intensifying as he cleared the landing. Hallway lay in shadow, the fading light from the master bedroom illuminating the crude lines of familiar script pissed onto the opposing wall—

MINE

—and soaking the huddled form below them.

Jesus Fuck, Kit.

Grim's nostrils flared, his stomach clenching with rage. He

swallowed the howl of anguish searing up his throat, pushing his cat down again and fighting the urge to rend the word to dust and spray everything with his own musk—

—MINE!—

Calm the fuck down!

"You here to piss on me, too?"

Grim's cat retreated, cowering from her voice. It was a study in controlled rage, her eyes boring into him from the shadows.

See, fuckwad? Let me handle this.

He approached her slowly, holstering his gun, and knelt down, a scant foot between them. Vomit crusted her hair, and her hoodie was drenched in piss. He reached out to her, and she flinched back, sending a knife through his heart. Something was wrong with her face. Grim swallowed the lump in his throat.

"No, Kitten, I'm here to take you home."

She laughed, the sound scraping from her like dead branches over a car door. "Why? So you can lock me in a room? That filthy motherfucker, *my father*, was waiting for me. He spat in my mouth, Grim. He wants me to turn into a monster like him—" She buried her face against her knees, hugging her legs tighter, shoulders hunching as she wept.

—KILL—

Yeah. Kill. But she comes first.

[SURPRISE]

Shut up. "Not possible. Reaper's his own special flavor of fucked-up. Most shifters aren't like that. Come on, let's get you out of here." He reached for her again, and this time she didn't pull away. Fur surged down his nape at the feel of her piss-soaked hoodie.

ENOUGH! Jesus, you're gonna make this worse. Look, let me get her somewhere safe—

—Mine!—

Not until Reaper's dead.

—YESSS—

"You fight with it, don't you?" She'd raised her head and was watching him like he was about to pull an *Exorcist*. A livid bruise darkened her cheek.

That motherfucker.

[RAGE]

I got this!

"I—yeah." He shrugged out of his jacket, seething, and held it open. "I need you to take off the hoodie and put this on." Kit's hands fisted the material at her throat. "Come on, it's disgusting, and my cat… please, Kit, just put on the fucking jacket."

Her lips flattened, but she pulled some shit out of her pockets, then unzipped it with trembling hands. Grim looked away, trying to ignore the way her tits strained against her tee, nipples rock-fucking-hard—

—Mmmm—

Christ, so was he.

Not the time, asshole. His jacket jerked as she slid her arms into the sleeves, pulling her hair out of the neck to fall around his cut's MC patch.

"You got all your stuff?" His voice cracked. Fuck, she looked right in his cut.

She nodded, inhaling his leather, cheeks pink even in the hallway's twilight, her scent subtly changing…

Fuck, she was getting off on his scent.

His cock went rigid.

—wants us—

Shut the fuck up. "Hold on." He pulled her against him, not able to meet her eyes when her ass brushed across his erection. Her blush got deeper. Grim picked her up, trying not to wince. Fuck his cock and fuck these fucking ribs…

Her arms banded around his neck as he stood. "What's wrong? Are you hurt? You know, I can walk…"

"I'm fine, and you shouldn't have to," he grumbled. Even

with pain like fire burning up his right side, and Grapple's piss making his eyes water, he didn't want to let her go.

Ever.

—ours—

Reaper dies first.

[SATISFACTION]

Her eyes searched his face, concern etching her brow. Damn, she was beautiful. He wet his lips, mouth abruptly dry. "Let me take care of you, Kit."

"Why? You don't even know me."

She was right, so why did it feel like he did? The answer rolled off his tongue before he could stop it.

"Because you're my mate."

Fuck. Did he just say that?

—purring—

[SATISFACTION]

Shit.

But damned him if it wasn't true.

Her breath caught, and she hid her face against his shoulder. Grim tightened his grip on her, navigating down those sketchy fucking steps to the front door as sobs wracked her body.

They'd done this to her. To his mate.

Jesus Christ, she was his mate.

[SMUG]

Wise it. "I'm gonna fucking kill them." That motherfucker had taken away her choice, just like he'd taken away so many of Grim's. A focused rage ignited in his belly. Reaper wasn't gonna get away with it. Not this time.

She cried harder.

—make them suffer—

Yes.

Grim kissed the top of her head and cradled her close, rocking. The roar of engines shattered the moment. Kit went still. "It's okay, I called them."

"For me?" she sniffled.

"Yeah, baby, for you." Wasn't a hundred percent true, but fuck if he was gonna tell her about Mike and Pete. He shouldered through the door to meet the cages coming up the drive.

Stitch and a full crew of twelve with Deuce at the helm were waiting for him when he splashed out of the mire.

Jaws dropped. All eyes on Kit wearing his cut.

—*Mine!*—

Grim bit back a growl. *They know, shithead. That's why they're staring.*

"Orders?" Stitch asked, trying to play it off.

"You got the car keys, baby?" he murmured. She fished them out, and Grim ignored the incredulous look on Deuce's face when he tossed them over. His best friend caught them, opened his mouth like he was about to say something, then just shook his head.

Whatever. "Take the car to the club. Rest of you check under the porch." Grim said, holding Kit tighter than he probably had to. His ribs sure as hell thought so but fuck them. "And look in the basement. I want this shithole razed when you're finished. Burn the fucking thing to the ground."

"Deuce, you good?" Stitch asked.

"Never fuckin' better." He glanced at Kit and shot Grim a thumbs-up, already directing the crew.

Stitch jerked his chin at MK's SUV and started walking. "Hop in, you're not getting that stink in my truck. There's a blanket in the back. Wrap your girl, we're going to the vet."

A growl rumbled through Grim's chest, and Stitch rolled his eyes.

"Suck it up, you go back to the club smelling like that and ain't no good comin' of it."

Damn it, but the fucker was right. "You gonna be civil?"

"S'up to Doc, now, ain't it?" Stitch muttered.

"I'm not hanging out to listen to you two—"

Kit's grip around his neck turned to banded steel. "Please don't leave me," she whimpered.

"No, baby. I'm not going anywhere," Grim said, ignoring Stitch's pointed look in the rearview.

—ours—

A flush of heat shot through him. Shit was a real possibility, and if Kit turned during the full moon tomorrow, there was no way he was ever letting her go.

[SMUG SATISFACTION]

Fuck off, asshole, that's a big if.

And if she didn't? Yeah, neither he nor his cat wanted to think about that.

CHAPTER SIX

KIT SNUGGLED AGAINST GRIM, cheek pressed to his shoulder, watching the stark outline of trees flitting past the moon as they drove. She shivered, and he pulled the scratchy blanket closer to her chin.

Taking care of her.

And she *liked* it.

Too much. The only person that'd ever given a shit, no strings attached, was Chanté, and that was a straight-up case of them against the world. Neither one of them fit, but by some strange twist of fate got along like proverbial peas and carrots.

So what was Grim's deal? She burrowed farther down into his jacket, inhaling deep. Damn if she didn't still want to roll around in that smell. But what did he want with her? Man was gorgeous and the heir apparent of his MC. He didn't need her or her baggage, especially when that baggage was Reaper.

Grim had to want something, other than getting his dick wet. Plenty of mollys would be lined up for that, and if her sack-of-shit father had been on the up and up about being his uncle?

No. Just fucking no.

None of this was real. Nope. Not happening to her.

Nope. Nothing is happening at the moment, but tell me you do not feel this man's cock against your ass every time we go over a bump. That could be happening. Make it so, Number One!

And now her vagina was a *Star Trek* fan. She bit back a groan.

Oh, please. Like you don't know whatever this is with Grim is happening, and you want more. Kit shivered again, unable to deny it.

He held her tighter. "Damn, we gotta get you warm. Heat go any higher?" he asked the grizzled brother driving. Man was a Jerry Garcia clone, and not one from the Grateful Dead's hey-day.

"S'already on full blast, and I'm sweating my balls off up here. Five more minutes. Doc's there now makin' sure you and your girl got everything you need."

She wasn't his girl, but Grim didn't argue, just grunted like he wasn't particularly thrilled about the statement, then kissed the top of her head like she was.

He'd been doing a lot of that since he found her.

… Because you're my mate…

But him saying that didn't make any sense, did it? She'd never shifted, so how would he know? A desperate yearning she didn't understand filled her chest. Could it be real?

Oh, it's real, girl. As in those big, tattooed arms wrapped around you, hand in your hair, all pressed up against his iron chest, without one damned excuse left not to get you some, real.

And her libido was officially out of control.

Nope. Not going there, especially if he was blood.

So find out, chickenshit. Ask the man.

Ugh.

"Is Reaper really your uncle?"

He tensed beneath her. "No. Why, what'd he say?"

"Nothing worth hearing." Kit shrugged, more relieved than she should be and totally not satisfied with his answer. "Why'd he say that, then?"

"Grim's mother, Abigail, was Reaper's queen," the driver said when it became obvious he wasn't going to elaborate.

Kit's brow furrowed at the term. A queen was like an alpha molly if she remembered right. The MC hadn't had one when she was growing up, which was one of the things she remembered her mother griping about, though not why…

"Was a damned tragedy when Abigail passed whelping," the driver went on. "Reaper adopted her boys."

"You have brothers?" Kit asked.

"Yeah." Grim glared at the driver through the rearview. "One of them pissed on you."

"*That's* your brother?" No way would she have thought that behemoth and Grim were related. Dude was huge and looked like he came out the ass end of a troll.

Grim just grunted, a muscle in his jaw ticking.

Whelp. Guess that's that. Kit settled back against him, her eyes caught by the fat silver orb just cresting the distant hills, not quite full.

Would be tomorrow night.

And then she would shift.

Maybe.

Saliva, blood, or semen. Any could instigate the change. Wasn't a given. Maybe she was one of those immune to the enzymes in shifter saliva.

Though Lord only knew what other communicable diseases were in that gelatinous glob that'd hit the back of her throat.

Her stomach cramped, and she lunged for the window, rolling it down and spattering vomit down the side panel.

"Jesus fucking Christ," the driver muttered, pulling over. "That's gonna be hell on MK's paint."

Grim snorted, one hand rubbing her back and the other holding her hair as she vomited.

Girl, he's holding your hair!

"Like he's ever gonna be able to get the smell of piss out of his upholstery."

"Fair point." The driver glanced at them through the rearview mirror. "We set?"

She collapsed against Grim, and he nodded, handing her a scrap of fabric to wipe her mouth. She took it gratefully—"Hey… This is my scarf."

"Yeah, I found it in the field when I was scoping out the house."

"No…" Her eyes welled up. "Y-you don't understand, Chanté gave it to me for luck, but it deserted me… shit, maybe I should've followed it…" Grim was looking at her like she was speaking Greek. "After I lost it, Reaper showed up, but then you came and brought it back."

His brow arched. Why was that so sexy? "Your luck."

"Yes."

"It's a scarf with dicks on it."

The man driving snorted, and she shot him a look.

"No," she patiently explained, "it's a good luck scarf with dicks on it."

"So… dicks are good luck?" He wet his lips and did that sexy eyebrow thing again.

"Just the ones on my scarf, asshole."

"Huh 'cause I was gonna say, if it works like one of those lamps, you're welcome to—"

The driver snickered, and she spun at him.

"You! Stay out of this!" Fucking men! She turned back to Grim. "That's a genie, not luck. They grant wishes, which I'm highly doubtful your dick is capable of."

He grinned. "Don't be so sure."

Oooh—that arrogant, son of a—Did she kill him or kiss him? Considering she'd just puked, it was likely she'd accomplish both…

Which means you'd never find out about those wishes.

Not that she wanted to.

Keep telling yourself that.

Fine. Raincheck on revenge. She fingered the silky fabric. It was stupid, but it felt like he'd given her a part of herself back.

"You know what, just forget it." She fumed, pushing off his lap to the other side of the backseat.

"Okay." Grim shrugged.

"No, it's not okay." Kit huffed, arms across her chest. "Don't patronize me."

"I wouldn't dream of it, Kitten."

"Stop calling me that."

His grin got bigger. "Stop liking it when I do."

"Right, kiddos, it's been fun." The driver threw the SUV into park. "We're here—get the hell out."

Kit eyes narrowed at them both before thunking the door open. They were on the outskirts of town, at a seedy strip mall she vaguely remembered. Probably because other than being condemned in the interim, it didn't look like it'd changed in the decade plus since she'd been there last.

A few cars littered the lot. Most didn't look drivable. Yellow tufts of weeds grew from the cracked pavement and all the storefronts were boarded up. The spray-painted tags had long since faded, and the entire place had an air of desuetude.

A severe, whip-thin older woman stood by the side door of what used to be a video rental place, the sign above vandalized to read "COCKBUSTER," complete with anatomical enlightenment.

Huh. Seemed like the universe was going with a theme tonight.

Kit stopped, trying to figure out how someone had gotten up there to tag it. Her head tilted. Maybe they'd hung upside down…?

Grim made a funny noise behind her.

"What?" she snapped, spinning with a huff.

He smirked at her rain boots. "Are those lucky, too?"

"No, just fabulous." But harder than hell to strut in.

She gave it her best shot, making her way to where the severe woman was dressing down the driver. Kit's footsteps slowed. Okay, not severe, more like uber-bitch. She was rocking a mohawk and wore an MC property cut, gun strapped to her thigh.

She was also pulling off a cool version of rabid.

"Fuck off, Stitch, I can smell pussy on you clear through the piss." She frowned, caught sight of Kit, and it slid to a scowl. "This her?"

"Who the fuck else would it be?" Stitch grumbled, fumbling with a vape. She directed her scowl back at him, and he muttered something, rubbing his nape.

"Triss," she barked over her shoulder, "you're babysitting."

Babysitting?

A girl a few years younger than Kit in surgical scrubs and Shirley Temple pigtails poked her head through the door, smiling ear to ear. She skipped—fucking skipped—over to Kit and caught her up in a hug.

"Welcome! Oh, I'm so happy you're here!"

Kit bit her lip, tearing up at the unexpected gesture.

"Save it, Triss," the woman snapped.

Triss rolled her eyes. They were the same vibrant green as uber-bitch's, but light years kinder. She clasped Kit's hand in hers. "Don't pay her any attention, or him, for that matter," she said shooting Stitch a long-suffering look. "Come on, let's get you cleaned up. I'm Triss. Those two are my parents. They're deeply in love, though you wouldn't know it."

Doc and Stitch snorted in tandem, not looking at each other. Instead, the woman's gaze narrowed in on Grim.

"Bring in the groceries and let Don Juan get rid of the stench mobile. Make it quick, there's ice cream."

"Yes, ma'am," Grim deadpanned.

Kit hadn't thought it possible, but the woman's scowl deepened as he went over to one of the less questionable cars and started hauling out brown paper bags.

Which was weirdly… domestic. She'd never thought about bikers getting groceries.

"He's one of the good ones," Triss stage-whispered, then squealed way too frickin' loud. "I can't wait for Nikki to find out he let you wear his cut! She's gonna die!"

Grim glanced up at them and grinned.

Who the fuck was—Wait, his cut? Kit looked down at the vest over his leather jacket. Claymore had never let her mother wear his. Only ol' ladies got to do that. Was that why they'd been staring at her back at the house?

Why would he—

… *Because you're my mate…*

That weird yearning was pressing against her chest again.

The girl tugged at her arm, and Kit let her shepherd her into the building. They passed through a desolate room filled with broken office furniture and drifts of garbage, into a stairwell leading down, and stopped in front of a banded steel door. Triss pulled out a keyring that looked like something a medieval jailer would keep at his belt and turned one of them into the lock.

Nothing happened.

"Security here's a thing." She smiled, nodding at a camera by the ceiling and giving it a wave. "You need both to get in… or out."

Kit's gut tightened. No… it was security… not locking her up, right?

Yeah, let's go with that.

Something metal clunked, and Triss pushed through the door into a sterile entryway with slots on the ceiling that looked suspiciously like murder holes. She repeated the key-and-wave process.

This time, the door opened up to a long hall that must

have run the length of the strip mall above. Rooms branched off on either side. The first few doors were open and outfitted with stainless steel tables and surgical implements, but the rest were closed off by thick steel slabs with rectangular cutouts at the bottom.

Something heavy slammed into one as they passed, and Kit jumped.

Triss waved her reaction away. "Don't mind that. Everything down here is designed to contain shifters. Rockwell's a sweetie, but this close to the full moon he gets extra."

"Extra?" Kit eyed the banded steel. What the hell was this place?

"Yep. Ah! Here's you, 21B." Triss grinned conspiratorially, flipping through her keys. "It has the best shower. Go on," she urged, unlocking the door and pushing it wide.

It was… cozy. Bigger than Kit's co-op rental in New York with a fraction of the charm. Everything was the same uniform gray as the concrete floor. A slightly darker scatter rug dotted the space in front of a cheap sofa and snap-together particleboard furniture. A TV was recessed in the wall behind a foggy layer of plexiglass.

She assumed that had something to do with the poorly spackled claw marks stippling the walls. Her throat constricted as she turned away.

A chipped Formica counter with a sink and a microwave ran along the opposing side of the room. Triss had skipped over and was showing her the contents of the cabinets like one of those *Price is Right* models.

"Towels are up here, paper products down there. If you want something real to eat, you gotta go to the galley, but there's ramen and those macaroni and cheese cups if you don't feel like peopling." She grinned at her again, grabbing two of the towels and motioning to a doorless entryway. "And through here's the bedroom."

It was as depressing as the rest of the place, but at least the bed was king-size… Though it looked like the sides would fold up as soon as someone sat in that permanent divot down the center. A pile of sweats was at its foot.

"Is there a laundry?"

Triss bit her lip. "There is, but speaking from experience, you're never gonna get that smell out—"

Kit's hands fisted, and she blinked back tears.

"—but we can try," the girl quickly amended far too cheerfully. "My mom swears by bitter orange and baking soda… I'll see what we can do. Just leave them outside the door, and I'll try and work some magic, okay?"

"Yeah." Kit wiped her eyes, God, she was stupid. Crying over a cheap tee and dollar-store yoga pants… but damn it, hadn't she lost enough? "Thank you."

Triss beamed at her and skipped to another doorless entryway. "And this is the bath."

She hadn't been kidding about the shower. It took up two-thirds of the room, a long bench seat running the entire length of the far wall, and it had at least four showerheads.

"Why's it so big? You could fit a Clydesdale in there."

Triss laughed, clapping her hands. "Not quite, but some of the brothers get huge when they shift. This is the room we have for when they have trouble coming back to two legs."

The lump was in Kit's throat again. "Is that a thing?"

"Only after severe trauma. Grim—" She slapped her hands over her mouth like she'd just blurted out nuclear code. "I didn't say that, okay?"

Hell to the fucking no, Kit wanted details, but the look on Triss's face… "Um… okay… so why no doors?"

The girl's grin was back. "Because cats don't have thumbs, silly."

Yup. Kit was definitely in an alternate universe. She opened her mouth to say something and the door in the next room banged open, slamming against the wall.

"Triss!" Doc yelled. "Dinner trays ain't gonna prep themselves!"

The girl's eyes rolled. "On it," she threw back over her shoulder, pigtails bouncing, then smiled at Kit. "Rockwell gets cranky when his dinner's late. I suppose the rest of the tour will have to wait, but Grim knows his way around—"

"Triss!"

She set the towels on the vanity and backed from the room. "We'll catch up later, it's gonna be so nice to have a new friend!"

A friend?

Kit stood there, mouth agape until the heavy steel door clunked shut, the silence in its wake claustrophobic.

She was alone, the acrid smell of piss reminding her why she was there.

Pull yourself together, Kit. Make a plan.

Right. A plan. For the first time in her life, there was only one line item.

Figure out what the fuck she was going to do.

Her legs gave out and she slumped to the floor.

What the fuck was she gonna do?

In less than twenty four hours, there was a strong possibility she was going to shift. And despite Grim's assertion of her being his mate, it was more likely she'd become one of *them*. A molly. Nothing but a place for some tom to shove his dick. They didn't have lives outside of the MC, surviving on whatever scraps the males threw to them.

Since Kit's mother, Marie, had been human, she wasn't technically a molly, but Claymore had treated her like one. Then when it soured between them, he wouldn't let her leave. Instead, he'd moved her out of the club and made her live in that house.

That's when Reaper had gotten Marie pregnant with Kit, and all of a sudden Claymore had been keen to play the doting father.

Kit frowned, hoping that they really had burned it down. Chanté's hoodie deserved a pyre.

She pulled her knees to her chin, her mother's smokey drawl in her ear…

"Saliva, blood, or semen, Kit Kat. Get any of theirs in you, and it'll trigger the change and turn you into one of them whore mollys."

Kit frowned, squirming at the kitchen table. She wasn't sure what all that meant, other than it was bad, and Claymore played with mollys a lot. Mama cried when he did.

"One of them toms starts sniffin' around your skirts, you run, you hear me?" She flipped the circle of dough over and started rolling it out.

"Should I go to my real daddy?" Mama had snuck her to see him a bunch, but he always made Kit's stomach feel queasy. She didn't like Reaper much, though Mama seemed to.

Her mama laughed. "Hell no, and Claymore ain't no better. All of them is monsters and'll put you in a box like this right quick." She paused her rolling to pinch Kit's chin, making her look up at her. "Your shine's too bright to waste on a man. You get yourself to the city. S'where they make dreams. Your Auntie Jojo said she'd take you in if somewhat happened to me."

"What's gonna happen to you, Mama?"

"Nothin' good, baby, I can promise you that."

And she's been right. Not long after, Reaper had put a bullet in her head, turning her into a vegetable. Auntie Jojo had taken her to see her mother a few times after, but it was crueler than standing over a grave.

Kit hadn't been back to see her in years.

Hope fucking sucked, and she was done with dreams.

Grim slunk down the hallway after Doc and Triss, wishing he was anywhere but here. Damned vet gave him the fucking creeps, the sanitary stench of bleach and all the monochrome put him on edge. He'd spent way too long in this place.

Specifically, in room 21B.

"Did you have to stick us in there?" he grumbled, setting the last of the groceries on the counter.

Triss put a hand on his arm. "Sometimes you have to lance a wound before it heals." He rolled his eyes, and she smacked him. "And it has the best shower. I bet she's in there, all soaped up waiting for you." Her eyebrows waggled.

"It's not like that."

"Yet," Stitch snorted from the table.

"Your dick get that memo?" Doc said at the same time.

They both swore and muttered something unflattering about each other.

Goddamn, their shit got old fast. "Yeah, but he doesn't read so well with one eye."

Stitch snickered into his ice cream, and Doc shot him a death glare.

They seriously needed to fuck and make up.

Doc set her sights on Grim. "Did you just make a joke? It was shit, but the fact that you put in effort—"

"Shoulda heard them in the car," Stitch muttered around his mouthful.

"Kit's good for him, I can already tell!" Triss bounced on the balls of her feet, hands clasped at her breast. Her Pollyanna bullshit got old fast, too.

Doc's brows furrowed, and she glanced at Stitch. Something other than vitriol passed between them.

His phone rang, killing the moment. "Yeah," he said, turning away.

Doc ran her hands down her thighs and sent her glare at Grim. "You break that girl's heart, and I'll beat the shit out of you."

"I don't plan on breaking anything."

Doc's mouth soured, and she snatched a towel, rage polishing the stove. "You toms never do."

"Oh please, Ma," Triss said, rolling her eyes. "Grim doesn't tom around, and he let her wear his cut. Brothers don't do that unless it's serious."

Shit, he had, hadn't he? At the time he'd just wanted her the fuck out of that hoodie, but the crew had seen her in it, and they were gonna think... Fuck, that was bullshit, he'd wanted them to see her in it. Wanted her to wear it. Grim ran a hand over his face. Might as well just fucking bite her and—

—YESSS—

No.

"It's not serious. She was cold. Kit's got no interest in becoming a shifter, and I've got none in forcing that decision. If it happens after what Reaper did, it happens, and if it doesn't... I'll cut her loose just as soon as that bastard's in the ground."

—NO! MINE!—

It's her fucking choice! I won't keep her here if she wants to go.

—growling—

Doc's eyebrow raised. "You serious?"

"About killing Reaper? Yeah. He's a fucking liability to the entire community. Asshole needs to be put down."

"I'll second that," Stitch said, pocketing his phone. "That was Wrench. Reaper's boys just raided Marie's facility. Shot the place up and took her. Media got video of a couple of them shifting. Feds is involved now. That ain't gonna sit well with the powers that be."

Fuck. Grim raked a hand through his hair. Paranormals weren't exactly in the closet, but there was an unspoken agreement for them to lay low. This clusterfuck would've just blown that to shit.

"Didn't Clay have ears at the bureau?" he asked.

Stitch grunted an affirmative. "MK's trying to do damage control, along with every other pack, pride, and whatever else in the area, MC or no, and the witches are pitching a fucking fit. Council's set a moot for tomorrow. You need to be there."

"They set a moot on the full moon?" Shit, if Kit was gonna go through the change, that's when it would go down. He couldn't leave her by herself…

Hello, elephant in the room.

"I'll stay with her," Triss said, uncharacteristically solemn.

"No. She's my responsibility."

Stitch's eyebrows just about shot off his forehead. "Since when?"

"Thought you just gave her your cut 'cause she was cold," Doc snapped.

Grim's hands fisted in his pockets. "She was."

"Bullshit. And if you leave her to go through her change alone, you'll lose her." Doc threw down her towel. Damn. She would know better than anyone.

Grim swore, turning to Stitch. "When and where?"

"Some club in the city, Meat Packing district. Moot's set for eleven AM… you might be able to get in and out with her before moonrise, but it's gonna be close."

Damn it all to hell, but Grim would take close over impossible any day. "Then that's what we do. Put together a crew and keep MK out of it."

Stitch pulled out his vape, lips pursing. "Any particular reason?"

"Yeah. I'm not convinced someone didn't tip Reaper off that we were gonna be at that club, and Kit said he was waiting for her at the house."

The man's eyebrows went even higher. "You think MK's the rat?"

Grim shook his head at the incredulity in Stitch's voice. "All I know is him and Clay got into it more than once over Nikki. He was less than fucking thrilled about me marking Kit, and Pete and Mike are both dead after I had him give them the order to tail her. Now Nikki's flaunting a bite I didn't give her, and Reaper's up my ass every time I turn around. Right before I broke it off with her, bitch said some shit about her options opening up if I got put down. I've no fucking clue if any of it's related, but I'd be stupid not to consider the possibility."

"I've always hated that whore," Triss said, shocking the shit out of everyone. "What? It's true. She's a horrible person… though I do envy her manicure. Girl can rock a gel tip."

"Only you, Triss, only you," Doc muttered, looking heavenward. "But I ain't gonna complain about Grim pulling his head out of her ass. Nikki's not queen material, and the MC wouldn't survive her posturing."

"Much as I hate to, I agree," Stitch said on an exhale, tapping his vape. "That shit she pulled with Miser's ol' lady? He's callin' for a vote over it. Wants Nikki's ass thrown out of the club. It's gonna get ugly."

—growling—

Grim winced. Ugly wasn't the word. "She's gonna blow shit up."

"Regardless, we gotta bring it to church. Table will swing in your favor, but the rest of the MC won't, and you ain't got the patch to override 'em."

Or enough support to rectify that problem. "When the fuck is that supposed to go down?"

"It's set for Monday, on account of the moot. You need to step up while you're there, Grim. Come clean about all the shit we talked about and make it clear to the council you're serious about taking prez and overseeing the region's business like Clay did. If they're backin' you, chapter'll fall in line."

Grim rocked on back his heels, frowning at his boots. "And if they don't?"

"They will. Get your fucking paperwork in."

He snorted. Sure, they would. Christ, this was a fucking mess.

"Go tend to your girl, Grim," Doc muttered. "I'll fill out the shit for the council. Cards is gonna fall the way they're gonna fall, and there ain't dick to be done about it tonight. This is the part where you focus on what's most important."

Grim rapped his knuckles on the counter and swore, the truth to that statement a painful ache in his chest. When the fuck had that happened?

Did it matter? What was most important didn't fucking want him.

CHAPTER SEVEN

THE DOOR to the hall slammed open, and Kit's head jerked up from her knees. She blinked and rubbed her eyes. Damn, how long had she sat there feeling sorry for herself?

"Kit?" Grim's voice came from the other room, along with the sound of heavy boots being toed off and shit hitting the counter.

"Um, yeah, in here—"

His long, lean frame blocked the light from the kitchen as he stepped into the open doorway, shirtless, his hands busy at his belt. He drew up short when he saw her. "You haven't showered?"

Stupidly, she stared at the hard planes of his body. "I... what happened to you?"

His torso was one huge bruise beneath a sculpted canvas of tattooed tribal art, the right side an ugly conglomeration of swollen black and green. His expression went hard. "Never mind about me, your lips are fucking blue. Come on, it's big enough for us both in there."

He moved past her to the bathroom, shucking off his jeans. They hit the tile with a wet plop, lying in a sodden puddle, along with his briefs. Kit stared at them, desperately trying to ignore the shower kicking on, and the fact he was in there, under the water, naked as the day he'd—

Christ on a fucking cracker. Her throat got tight. "You want me to shower… with you…"

Crickets.

Maybe he couldn't hear her over the spray.

She should look… *I mean, just to see if he heard me. It'd be rude to repeat myself, right?*

Girl, you know you just wanna see what he's packin'.

She licked her lips. Yeah. And that…

Holy fucking hotness.

He'd chosen the shower head closest to the door, giving her a full Goddamned frontal. His tattooed arms were raised, biceps bulging, eyes closed, hands buried in his wheaten hair turned dark in the hot spray. Water cascaded over his face, down his sculpted chest, to a line of curls bisecting his adonis belt, and a pierced cock that she was pretty sure would indeed grant wishes.

He blew out a mouthful of water, head back, his hands dropping to cup his balls and stroke over his shaft, washing himself. Kit's mouth went dry.

"Enjoying the show?"

Her eyes flicked up to meet his. Bastard was smirking. *Yeah, you just got caught… now whatcha gonna do about it?* Kit's jaw snapped shut, and she stood to grab a toothbrush from the sink.

"Depends, what's it called?" she asked, squirting far too much toothpaste on the bristles. "*Shameless Exhibitionist Uses All the Hot Water*? I'll pass, thanks."

Liar.

He laughed and turned around to grab a bottle of shampoo from the bench. Kit spun around fast, biting the toothbrush so hard she swore it cracked as she ogled him in the mirror. Sweet baby Jesus… That full back tattoo and God*dayum*, fuck quarters, man had an ass that would bounce an Olympic medal.

And I'll be damned if he doesn't win the gold…

He grinned over his shoulder at her reflection. "If you're that worried about the hot water, you better get it while you can."

Yeah, hurry up and scrub those teeth, Kit, then go get you some.

Quiet you. She spat, her thighs squeezing together. She needed to get her vagina a muzzle. Ugh! Why did he have to be so damn fine?

Whatever. He was right, the shower was huge and even with her in there, there'd be a good six feet between them. Plenty of room, and the filth on her was abruptly unbearable. She wriggled out of his jacket and laid it on the vanity, her skin prickling in the steamy air. Boots came off, and then her yoga pants… She snuck another look at Grim.

He was soaping up his hair, dick bobbing, not a care in the damn world.

Fine. Two could play at that game, but there was no way she was getting naked in front of him. She took a deep breath and walked into the shower, still wearing her tee and panties.

Despite the steam, the water was cooler than she normally liked, but she wasn't complaining. She dipped under the spray and snagged a bottle of shampoo off the bench. Ugh, her hair was a nasty tangle, bits of funk peppering the floor as she scrubbed, rinsed, and repeated. It was gonna take more than one go to get it clean.

She turned to rinse again, and her eyes sprang open at a growl.

"If you left that shirt on to maintain your modesty, it's not fucking working." Grim gritted out, one hand on the wall, the other on his cock, bent forward like someone had punched him in the gut.

Kit looked down. Shit. Her pale pink tee had gone translucent, and her pebbled nipples were clearly visible right down to her areolas.

So, work it. You want some, and with a dick that hard, he's game. What's stopping you from cashing in on some heavy petting? Daddy dearest's nasty gift solved your moratorium on saliva…

You know what? Her vagina was right. She still didn't know what she was gonna do, but right about now she sure as hell knew what she wanted, and it looked like he wanted to play ball.

"What's the matter, not enjoying the show?" She smirked.

"Oh, I'm enjoying it, but knowing there's no audience participation is killing me."

———

—WANT—

Grim bit back a groan, struggling to breathe normally. God help him, he'd tried to keep his mouth shut, but seeing her ogle his cock had blown away every good intention he'd ever had.

And Jesus Christ, those fucking tits were just begging to be sucked…

No. I'm not gonna touch her. Not gonna touch her. Not gonna—

Kit turned her back to him and peeled that fucking tee up over her head.

—Mmmm—

His balls cinched tight, pre-cum coating this hand. Christ, what was he? Thirteen?

"Not sure where you got that idea," she said, flicking her hair forward. "I was just about to ask you to wash my back."

Another long, slow line dripped from his tip. "Y-your back?" His voice cracked.

She wanted him to touch her.

"Yeah, you know, that bit between my shoulders and my ass?"

—laughing—

He swallowed, hand tight on his junk. *Wise it, fucker.*

Kit gathered her long hair to the side, juicy ass peeking

out from black boy shorts, suds caught in all the right places, water streaming down the sinful curves of her body.

Jesus. Fucking. Christ.

She glanced at him over her shoulder, raising an eyebrow, then dangled one of those scrubby mesh things from a fingertip. "Better hurry, before the water gets cold."

Hurry? Fuck that, he was gonna take his time—

She bent the fuck over to grab a bottle from the bench.

Grim bit his knuckle so hard he heard it crunch.

—wants us—

No, she… fuck, does she?

Kit stood, soaping up the scrubby, her bare tits so fucking ripe. Saliva pooled in his mouth. "What's the matter, Pussycat? You shy?"

A growl rumbled in his chest. "Pussycat?"

She shrugged, failing to hide her grin. "Yeah, if you get to call me Kitten, then I guess you're my Pussycat."

Grim swallowed hard. Sweet Lord, he'd be her everything.

He ventured closer to take the scrubby. She passed it over and put her palms flat on the wall, planking out her body.

"Don't be afraid to do it hard."

—YESSS—

No! He took a step back. "Shit. Kit, I can't…"

"You can't what? Wash my back?" Her voice flowed out in a teasing lilt, the smile in it going straight to his throbbing dick.

—laughing—

—yesss wants us—

No, Goddamn it! Grim slung the scrubby onto the bench and ran a heavy hand down his face, flicking water from his scruff. "No." He laughed. "I can't wash your back because I can't fucking touch you without—without *touching* you."

Motherfucker, he so wanted to touch her.

She spun to face him, cocking her head and popping a hip,

all kinds of pissed off, and those Goddamned tits, taut nipples the perfect shade of rose—he licked his lips.

"Why not?"

—?—

Fuck! "Because you don't want it!" he yelled, throwing his hands up.

Her face went hard, and she stepped so close those peaked pink nubs brushed his chest. Grim bit back a groan, nails cutting into his palms.

"You know what I want, Grim? How about every asshole male in my life to stop telling me what I want. What's 'best for me.' " She finger-quoted. "I fucking hated it when Claymore did that shit, and I'd advise you to quit while you're ahead, so shut the fuck up and kiss me!"

—YESSS—

What? He stood stock-still, staring at her.

Kit rolled her eyes. "God, men really are useless." She grabbed the back of his neck and dragged his head down to meet her lips.

—laughing—

She pressed her mouth against his, so fucking soft, giving and taking, her breath mint and molten fucking need. She softened against him, slick thighs caging his leg, stretching up on her tiptoes to follow him as he pulled back, his palms against her cheeks, thumb skating over that fucking bruise and searching her eyes.

"You sure?" The question was jagged sugar rumbling from his throat.

"I'm not sleeping with you, but saliva's on the table," she breathed, giving his nipple ring a tug. He groaned, the sensation shooting straight to his balls and drawing them up.

"I can work with that," he murmured, nipping her lip. Goddamn, work? He was gonna feast... "Promise me something first."

Her eyebrow canted, and his arm circled her waist, jerking her against him.

"You don't run from me."

"Ever?"

He chuckled at the wicked glint in her eye. "Not without consequences."

"Will I like them?"

"I know I will. I've been dreaming about spanking this ass." His hand cracked down on one of her cheeks, and her pupils blew out, steam thick with the scent of her arousal, her warm honey coating this thigh.

Oh, fuck yeah… "Hands on the wall, Kitten. You wanted me to wash your back."

She bit her lip and set her palms against the tile, head hanging low.

Grim gripped his throbbing cock, swearing. Jesus Christ, she was sexy as fuck. He grabbed the scrubby, swirling suds over her silken skin. Lavender and orange biting through Grapple's claim.

Not enough.

His head dipped, nose skating over the pale flesh of her spine, an angry rumble in his chest.

—Mine!—

She tensed. "Do you still smell it?"

"Yeah." He soaped up the scrubby again. *And I fucking hate it.*

"Scrub harder."

"It doesn't—It doesn't work like that," he muttered, laving around her nape. His canines elongated, the urge to bite her overwhelming.

—Mark her!—

No.

"Then how does it work?"

"Move under the water."

She sidled beneath it, and he kicked her feet wide, stepping between her splayed legs. The weeping tip of his cock brushed against her, water washing his seed away. What he wouldn't give to paint her with it, to lick it from her quivering folds, then feed it to her, warm from his mouth… His dick jerked, and he grabbed her hip, pulling her against him and sliding the root of his cock along her crack. He needed to calm the fuck down, but Jesus fuck, she felt good.

—ours—

"Grim?"

"Mmm?"

"How does it work?"

"Umm…" He took a half-step back, sudsing slow circles around her panty-clad hips. Those needed to fucking go. "It's gotta be covered, and I'm not pissing on you."

"That's the only way?"

"Didn't think other was on the table." He skated the scrubby around to her stomach and ribs, his knuckles brushing the underside of her breast. "Unless you want my cum on you."

She gasped at his hand moving up to cup her breast, fingers scissoring over a nipple and tugging. Her back arched, ass pressing against him.

"Is on me the same as in me?" She whimpered as he pinched her into a trembling point.

"No, but… Goddamn, you feel so fucking good." He smacked the shower head to the side and dropped to a knee, chucking the scrubby aside.

"What are you doing?"

The slight tremor in her voice shot straight to his dick. "Taking these off." He knelt behind her, a nail lengthening to a claw and slicing through the side seam of her panties. Kit's thighs shook as they slipped down her leg. Grim gripped her ass cheeks, squeezing and spreading them. He inhaled along her slit, and she trembled.

"Goddamn. You smell like fucking heaven…" He parted

her lips with his thumbs, revealing her little pink hole, dripping cream. His tongue flicked out, and he groaned at her cry. Fuck, she was delicious. "You wanna be a good girl for me, don't you, baby?"

"Yes—Oh!"

His hand slapped down onto her ass, the sound amplified by the dewy tile. He rubbed her pinked cheek, his dick hard as steel. "Mmm. You like that?"

"I-I don't know…"

He nipped at her bottom, fingers dipped between her thighs. Jesus fuck, she was wet. So fucking wet. "Your pussy says you do. Ask me for another."

She arched her back, chasing his touch. "Please, Grim… Oh!"

He spanked her other cheek, the scent of her arousal thickening. Fuck, her ass bloomed so pretty… His palm fell again, and she raised up on her tiptoes with another cry. He laved over the marks, licking and kissing, working his way to her rosebud. She jerked to her tiptoes at the pointed pressure of his tongue.

"Damn, you're fucking gorgeous. Tell me what you like, Kitten. Let me please you…"

Fuck, he so wanted to please her, to feel her come on his fingers, his mouth…

"I don't know."

His bows furrowed as he sat back on his heels and flicked water from his eyes. "What do you mean?"

"Just what I said," she huffed. "Do you have any idea how nerve-wracking it is to go on a date and trying to figure out if the guy you're with is a shifter? It was just easier not to."

It was— "What?"

Kit laughed, dropping her hands from the tile to grab her ankles and looked at him upside-down through the V of her legs, her hair an inky puddle between her feet. He groaned at her swollen pussy on display. "I'm a virgin, Grim. Twenty-three and never been kissed until tonight, so, thanks for that."

How the— "Are you fucking serious?"

She stood back up, and pirouetted to face him, her eyebrow arching. "Is that a problem?"

"No one's ever touched you?"

Kit rolled her eyes. "Correct."

She'd be his. Totally fucking his.

—*ours*—

Whatever. He stalked closer, pinning her against the wall, his breath coming fast. "You touch yourself?"

A blush stained her cheeks. "Well, yeah, sometimes."

He ran a hand over his face, swallowing a mouthful of water. Damn, it was hot in here. "Show me."

Those beautiful brown eyes went wide. "Sh-show you?"

"Yeah, I want you to sit right there and show me how you do it."

She glanced at the bench and then back at him. "I—"

"Spread your legs and play with that pretty pussy for me, Kitten."

She hesitated, but sat on the bench, a moment later running a tentative hand down her stomach, through her trimmed curls—

"Wider, I wanna see."

She bit her lip, and then hooked her heels on the edge of the bench. "Like this?"

"Yeah, baby, just like that." His hand slid over his dick. "Now spread your lips and show me how wet you are."

Fuck, she was soaked. She strummed across her clit, her hole contracting and spilling cream. Grim licked his lips, thumb rubbing pre-cum from his crown.

"Show me how you finger yourself."

Her hand slid lower, teasing herself with a fingertip. "Only if you show me how you do it, too."

"Yeah?" He gripped himself tighter. "You wanna watch me stroke my cock?"

Her breath caught, staring as he ran his hand from root to tip, twisting. Kit's fingers grew bolder, disappearing to the second knuckle. Goddamn, he wanted to drive himself in there balls-deep, claiming her as his.

"You fuck yourself with a vibrator?"

"Yes," she breathed, her gaze not leaving him working his dick.

"It as big as me?"

She shook her head, blushing again. Christ, that was adorable.

"You fuck yourself with it hard or soft?"

"Both."

"How would you do it now?"

"Hard."

His balls tightened. Jesus fuck, she was gonna kill him. He dropped to his knees between her thighs, needing to worship, wanting to defile. "Gimme a taste."

She held out her fingers, and he sucked them into his mouth, her sweet musk coating his tongue…

Not enough.

He caged her wrists, raising them above her head. "Lie down." His body slid to cover hers beneath the spray, climbing above her. "Mmm. Now come here and taste how delicious you are." His mouth found hers, tongue pressing against the seam of her lips. She opened for him, gasping when he thrust it into her, exploring her mouth, then chasing his tongue to explore him.

"Fuck, you like that, don't you?"

She moaned. "So much…" Her leg skated up his thigh, opening her core to him.

His breath caught. "You said no sex."

"Maybe I lied?" She shrugged, so fucking cute.

"Maybe this pussy's just needy." He chuckled, his hand slid between her legs, fingers delving into her slick folds. "That better, baby?"

"Oh God, yes..." Kit moaned, back arching off the bench, offering up those luscious tits. He latched onto one, sucking hard, tip stiffening against his tongue, her walls fluttering around his fingers. He pumped them slow, reveling in her moans. So fucking responsive to his touch.

She rode his hand, taking everything he was giving her, skin flushed, whimpering...

"More..."

"Yeah? You want me to fuck this tight little pussy? Fill it up with my cum?"

—*YESSS*—

A burst of honey soaked his hand, even as her brow furrowed. He took away his fingers, moving to slick the base of his cock against her, kissing her hard and rolling her nipple between his thumb and forefinger. Fuck he wanted her, but no way in hell was he gonna force it, no matter how bad he wanted to sink into her tight little cunt.

"Please, Grim..." she pleaded between kisses, "I was so close..."

And Goddamn he loved hearing her beg.

—*DO IT!*—

No.

"Stop teasing!" she gasped.

"Shh... Keep your hands above your head."

His lips fell to her throat, nipping and sucking a long, wet line to her breasts, filling his mouth with her glorious rose-tinted nipples, tormenting them to points until she sobbed.

"Oh God, Grim, please...

"You my good girl, Kitten?"

"Yes!"

"Then ask me to eat your pussy."

"E-eat my pussy…"

He pulled her to the edge of the bench and spread her thighs wide, parting her lust-puffed lips. His tongue swept up her slit to swirl around her swollen nub, teasing and sucking. Her hips rocked against him, and he chuckled. "So fucking needy. You want my fingers in your cunt again, baby?"

"Yes…"

He traced around her hole like she had. His forearm pinning her across the waist, watching her pussy quiver for him.

She bucked against his hold. "I said stop teasing me!"

"Stop getting so Goddamn wet when I do." He slowly pushed a finger in, her walls a velvet vise throbbing around him, trying to suck him in deeper. Christ, she was gonna strangle his dick.

She keened. "More… I need more…"

Yeah, he'd give her more.

"Shhh… be patient…" His lips fastened around her clit, finger curving upward, rocking into her. Adding another finger and scissoring deep. Kit's breathing sped, her thighs flexed.

"Oh God, Grim, I'm—"

Her pussy spasmed and sweet, sweet honey coated his hand.

—FEAST—

His cat growled, and Grim threw her legs over his shoulders, devouring her.

Her hands fisted his hair. "Oh, oh! No. No more, no—Oh, wait, yes, yes—"

———

Kit came again, hard, her vision going white, hips lifting off the bench to ride Grim's face. He chased after her orgasms, feasting on her until she sobbed, thighs chafed from his scruff, her body wrung out and limp.

He kissed her softly. "You're so Goddamned beautiful when you come for me."

Blissed out, she tangled her fingers in his hair. "Mmm. Your turn, Pussycat."

Grim sat back on his heels, gripping his dick. The crown was an angry red, tip weeping as he stroked. She licked her lips, wanting to know what he tasted like.

A guttural moan came from his throat. "Don't look at me like that."

"Like what?"

"Like you wanna eat me."

"What if I do?" She slid off the bench to the floor, leaning against it beneath the warm spray and traced his throbbing tip with a finger to play with the piercing at the edge of his crown. His cock bucked, and he bit back a groan, retreating. "Don't you want me to touch you?"

His Adam's apple bobbed. "So fucking bad… but it's not a good idea."

It wasn't. But at the moment, she didn't particularly care.

"Mark me."

He went still.

"Like you said. With your cum."

His tongue slid over his lips, pupils slitting, then snapping back to round. And repeat. She smirked. He was fighting with himself again. She put her back to him, ass on her heels, nesting her arms on the bench and cradling her head.

"Please, Grim, I want you to."

The silence between them stretched, water hissing against the tile, then his fingertips skated down her spine, and she shivered in anticipation.

"I-it'll mean something to me, Kit. To my cat. He'll—you'll be ours." His thighs bracketed hers, the long, thick length of him sliding between her cheeks. "Do you want to be ours?"

She moaned at the feel of his cock slicking against her ass, something in her straight-up preening, that yearning in her chest about to burst. God, it was insane, but—

She did.

"Yes." Her voice husked out like it wasn't her own.

"What if you don't change?" he murmured, an arm banding her waist, his hips making one long, languorous thrust against her, his cock leaving a slick line down the base of her spine. "Will you leave me?"

"Only if you try to make me stay."

His forehead dropped to her shoulder, hair tickling her skin, cock pumping slow between their bodies. He peppered kisses up her throat, soothing the roughness of his scruff, teasing her with his teeth, elongated and sharp against her pulse.

"I wanna claim you with my bite so fucking bad, Kit," he panted. "Shove my cock deep inside your pussy and barb you when I come. I wanna hear you yowl when I fill your belly with my seed and breed you. Please you so you never want to leave. Worship you as my mate, my queen..." His voice cracked. "Fuck, I wanna give you everything."

Take. It.

Could she? Her hips canted back, and she whimpered, a part of her needing desperately to believe him and simultaneously terrified by his words. That yearning in her chest had become a burn, a wanting so powerful it hurt. His breath was hot and fast on the shell of her ear, fingertips plucking at her breast, dropping to strum along her folds...

She moaned, so close to the brink again...

"That's what me marking you means. It's a promise, Kit. Tell me you want me like that, and I'll give it to you, but if you don't, I-I can't do this to either of us." His rhythm faltered, voice strained—

Take it, girl! Get out of your damned head and let him mark you!

Sweet baby Jesus, she was out of her Goddamned mind, but she wanted this man more than she wanted her next breath. More than her slim chance at humanity. She dropped her hand between her legs to give his heavy sac the gentlest of tugs, and he groaned, thrusting against her spine. "Mark me, Grim."

CHAPTER EIGHT

—MARK HER!—

Grim's eyes rolled as Kit's fingers smoothed along his sac. Jesus fuck… She'd said yes. He didn't know why, but right about now, he didn't give a shit.

He was marking her as his.

—ours—

Whatever.

His hand clamped onto her breast, fingers delving deeper inside her sweet, slick velvet, dick sliding along the thick trail of wetness it'd left. Her cunt quivered, so fucking close…

He threw his head back, lost in the feel of her. A tingle shot up his spine. "Fuck, baby, I'm gonna come—"

Colors burst across the insides of his eyelids, long ropes of his release painting her with molten desire. Her thighs clamped around his hand, cunt spasming as she moaned, wetness seeping past his fingers. *Fuuuck…*

—More—

Grim smirked. *Greedy fucker.* He fell onto his heels, dick iron again at the sight of his seed dripping down her back and along her ass crack. Grim swept it up, spreading it across her skin, kneading it into her nape, her breasts. Pinching it into her nipples and biting at her neck, a growl rumbling through his chest.

"Mine."

—ours—

"Mmm. Yours," she murmured, arching against him with a purr—

She was fucking purring.

He flipped her around to straddle his lap, studying her eyes.

"What?" She laughed, pulling away to tweak his nipple ring. Her pupils were still circles.

"You were purring."

Kit blanched. "I was?" She scrambled into the water, rinsing herself off.

Grim snorted, getting to his feet. "It's not gonna work that fast… and neither would what Reaper did. The moon triggers the first change."

"Well, it's midnight somewhere in the world!" she snapped, then sighed, scrubbing water over her face. "What am I gonna do, Grim?"

She looked so sad sitting there, knock-kneed beneath the cooling spray.

He pulled her to her feet and kissed her, switching the water off. "We'll figure it out later. I'm fucking starving. Let's dry off and get something to eat."

She cast him a sidelong smile as he wrapped her in a towel. Shit was scratchy as fuck. She needed something softer. "Will uber-bitch—I mean Doc, be there?"

He chuckled. "Yeah, probably."

"Then ramen sounds good."

"I'll go grab us something," he said, toweling off his face. A shave would wait until tomorrow… though fuck if he didn't like the way his beard burn looked between her thighs. "You feel okay?"

Kit followed his eyes and blushed. Damn, that was adorable. "Yeah, I'm fine… is it gone now? His mark?" She held the towel to herself and turned, pulling her hair away from her nape.

Grim stepped close, skating his nose up her throat and loving the goose bumps he left in his wake. "Mmm. Just me and you…" He dragged his teeth over her soft flesh, catching her look of desire in the foggy mirror. Had her pupils wavered? His arm circled her waist, and he nipped at her lobe.

"Soon, baby," he rumbled.

Her expression turned sly. "What will we do until then?"

"Mmm. Greedy." Grim kissed her shoulder and toweled the rest of the way off. "Not what you think. I gotta go into the city tomorrow. Your friend, Chanté, she's down there, right?"

Kit flipped her hair up into one of those towel turban thingies. "Yes…"

"I thought maybe you could hang out with her while I take care of stuff. My cell's on the counter. While I'm grabbing something to eat, why don't you call her? My code's 5-5-6-2-7-8."

She leaned against the vanity. "You know I'm gonna look through all your shit, right?"

Okay, maybe that hadn't been the best idea. Grim resisted the urge to glance in its general direction. Was there anything on there that'd fuck him over?

Probably, and too late now.

—idiot—

Thanks. "Go for it, if you don't mind waiving your right to plausible deniability." Her eyes widened, and he forced a grin, only kind of teasing. "I figured we could head down early, grab breakfast on the road, then be back before it gets dark—"

"You mean before I change… if I change." She bit at a cuticle.

"Kit, I—"

"Any chance I can get the purple suitcase from my car?" She glanced at the raggedy sweats he was pulling on. "Not that I'm ungrateful, but if I show up in those, I'll never hear the end of it."

He went into the other room to snag his phone. "Sure, lemme text Deuce..." *And delete as much shit as I can without being obvious...* He pulled up his text messages. "Shit."

"Problem?" she asked, not even trying to act like she wasn't craning to see the screen.

Grim bit his lip. "Yeah, I didn't see this one come in... it's from MK." The bodies had been ID'd. Pete and a couple of townie kids. So then where the fuck was Mike?

"I gotta make a call. Won't take long. TV remote's in the side table drawer. Gimme fifteen, ok?" He pulled on a tee and headed for the door.

"Sure, and hey, if there's beer, I'll take one."

"Will do."

The door to the room closed behind him, and he slumped against the wall, clunking it with his head and looking up. Jesus, that'd been close. MK's text hadn't been the only one, and Grim could only imagine what Kit would do if she'd unlocked his phone to find a pic of Nikki's pussy and a Face-Time request waiting for him. What the fuck had he been thinking making a deal with that bitch? Ceiling didn't have any answers, and what he was getting from his cat wasn't flattering or anatomically possible.

"Stop fucking up my paint," Doc snapped, headed to the galley with a stack of empty trays. She paused, looking him up and down with a smirk. "Somebody got some."

"Shut the fuck up." He scowled, pushing past her into the galley.

She snickered and damn him if his scowl didn't turn into a smile.

"You plan on chewing dinner with your own teeth after talking to Doc like that?" Stitch asked as Grim walked past him to the fridge. He was still at the table, working through a slab of lasagna thicker than the Bible.

"I'm giving him a pass. You'd think you'd recognize the look of a man who just claimed his mate," Doc said, placing the trays in the sink. "Oh, that's right, you were full of shit when you did."

Grim opened the fridge, rummaging. And cue reason seven thousand and six why he hated going to the vet. "I didn't claim her. Any more of that lasagna?"

"Full of shit, huh? That must explain the sudden urge to add more fiber to my diet," Stitch shot back.

"Now there's an idea. Suggest you try it in suppository form. Best way to insert it's on the end of my foot, delivered at high speed." She waved at a covered pan to her right, turning to do the dishes. "It's on the stove. What do you mean you didn't claim her?"

"Thanks." Grim ignored the question, flipping through his phone. *Delete, delete, delete... block Nikki... delete, delete...* He shot Deuce a text about grabbing Kit's luggage and some other shit... Thumbs up and an ETA of a half hour. Nice. "MK message you?" he asked Stitch.

"Yeah. We got eyes out, but no sign of the boy. Ain't like Mike to just up and disappear, neither."

Doc grabbed another dirty tray. "You think Reaper's got him?"

"That, or he saw somethin' that freaked him out enough to go to ground and stay there. You put tarragon in this, woman?"

"Just shut the hell up and eat the damned thing, Stitch," Doc bristled. "You're lucky I'm feeding your ugly ass anything."

"Must be that dick scarf rubbing off on me. And I was gonna say, it's delicious."

Doc huffed, failing to hide a smile. "The fuck is a dick scarf?" She looked at Grim. "Do I want to know?"

"Kit's lucky scarf," he said, pulling a clean tray from the stack and flicking the foil from the pan. Looked amazing.

Whatever the hell tarragon was, he was game. "It's got dicks on it."

"All righty, then. By your expression out in the hall, I'm assuming that luck extends to you, considering you smell like you took a bath between her legs."

I don't just smell like it, I did, and it was fucking glorious.

—ours—

Yeah… Grim paused, leaning against the counter, spatula in hand. "She asked me to cover Grapple's mark."

"And?"

"I did." He shrugged, trying to play it off, even though they knew what that meant for him.

Stitch fell back in his chair and Doc just stared.

Yeah, they knew.

"Your cat let you?" Stitch sputtered.

"He—I'm not pressuring her to turn. If Reaper's saliva doesn't do it…" Grim shrugged again. "Either way, she's our mate, and if she wants it, our queen."

"You can't have a—"

"Don't fucking say it," he growled at Stitch, fur bristling over his knuckles.

The man held up his hands, tipping back in his chair.

"He's not wrong, Grim." Doc's expression was pained. "That's why Clay never made Kit's mother, Marie, his equal. Council won't stand for a human in the position and if things don't fall the way you want tomorrow night—"

"Technically, she's only half human, and as far as I'm concerned, it's already done." And they could all kiss his hairy ass if they thought he was giving Kit up or relegating her to molly status. He poked at the top layer of cheese. "I'll deal with it when and if it doesn't happen. The current shit-storm Reaper stirred up's got precedence. You pull together a crew?"

Stitch ran a hand over his face. "Yeah. Usual suspects will be riding down. Supposed to be 'unseasonably warm.' "

"Sounds good." He shot another text to Deuce to bring his bike over while he was at it—

"Might wanna check if your girl's up for riding bitch before you sign her up."

Grim froze, staring at his screen. Another thumbs-up bubbled from Deuce. Shit, what if Kit wasn't into it?

"Why, Stitch, that's one of the only sensible things I've ever heard come out of your mouth," Doc said, smacking Grim out of the way and grabbing the spatula from him. "Stop mauling my hard work. Why the hell neither of you can manage to cut a straight damned line..." She plated the tray and shoved it at him with a couple of forks. "Here, take it. Go feed your girl, and I suggest you let her know about her mama while you're at it."

Shit. Yeah, that... "Yes, ma'am." He snagged the six-pack on the way out the door, pretty sure he was gonna need more than a couple of beers for that conversation.

———

"Damn, that stinks," Kit murmured, dumping the lot of her nasty laundry in the hall for Triss with one last mournful look at her Doc Martens. She didn't hold out much hope for their salvation, or for the rest of it.

She sighed. At least it wasn't a total loss. Her lucky scarf seemed to have made it through unscathed. She touched the damp fabric cinching up her hair. After she'd rinsed the mud off, it looked none the worse for wear.

The same couldn't be said about her borrowed sweats. They looked like they'd been picked out of a YMCA lost and found. Hopefully, Grim could get someone to deliver her suitcase.

Her stomach fluttered and she smiled, running a hand over the burn his scruff had left on her inner thighs. That was real. What they'd done... Damn, the things he'd done... She fanned herself. Man was no joke. The dudes in Chanté's pornos could learn a thing or ten.

Ugh. Chanté. Kit bit at her cuticle. Woman was gonna flay her ass for not calling sooner, good excuse or no. It was a conversation she was looking forward to and dreading in equal parts. Her bestie was way overprotective sometimes, and Kit had a feeling this was gonna be one of them.

At least she had a reprieve from that until Grim got back with dinner. Her stomach growled. Soon, hopefully. Sighing, she snagged the TV remote and flopped onto the couch, pulling at the neck of her borrowed tee.

Surprise, surprise, there wasn't cable. Of the three channels, one was some mega church service—hard pass on that— a 24-hour shopping channel hawking seriously creepy China dolls, and the local news. Some blonde chick was interviewing an old lady about a pet bingo night, whatever that was. Huh. The story sucked, but Kit did have to admit the way the reporter's bob stayed perfectly in place as leaves gusted by was riveting.

She rolled her eyes, ready to flick it off when the anchors came back on.

"Thanks, Jolene, what a great cause. I know where I'll be this Sunday after church." The anchor turned to his co-host with a cheesy smile plastered on his face. Man's threaded brows were just bizarre. "How about you, Sally?"

"Well, as much as I'd love to be there to benefit our furry friends, I'm going to be at the candlelight vigil being held for Sarah Becks, Justin Herd, and Peter Wygold, the victims in the latest spate of murders to rock our small town." The camera cut away, and their headshots flashed up on the screen.

One was Zits, that kid from the chapter house's gate.

The remote clattered onto the floor and Kit leaned forward. "What the hell…"

"The victims' remains were found earlier today, via an

anonymous source, at the long-condemned James's residence, in the foothills east of town. As you know, Brian, Nathaniel 'Claymore' James, a well-known figure in the local biker community, was brutally murdered earlier this month, and authorities are looking at a possible connection. Unfortunately, the investigation has been hampered by a suspicious fire at the property, which has been ruled as arson."

The screen flicked to a smoking ruin and then back to the newsroom.

"My, yes, Sally—I can see how that would complicate things. Such a tragedy all around. The thoughts and prayers of all of us here at Channel 19 are with the families and loved ones of the victims." The anchor faced the camera again, the shot zeroing in on him. "And in national news—Shifters. Are we safe? The answer may surprise you, after this commercial break."

"We should probably talk before you watch that," Grim said, standing in the doorway with a tray of food and a six pack.

Kit picked up the remote and switched off the TV. Her hands shook. "How about you give me one of those beers first. Zits and those kids are dead because of me, aren't they?"

Grim put the tray down on the coffee table, door clunking shut behind him. He cracked a beer and handed it to her. "Zits?" he asked, dropping onto the other side of the couch.

"Yeah, him and Pornstache were at the gate."

"You mean Pete." Grim snorted. "I asked MK to have them keep an eye on you after you stormed out of the clubhouse. If them dying's anyone's fault, it's mine."

"You were keeping an eye on me?" Her skin crawled, that was too close to how she'd lived under Claymore's thumb.

No, Grim's not like that…

"We knew Reaper was looking for you. I figured if he showed, one of them could give us the heads-up you were in trouble… but after a couple of hours they stopped checking in, which is why I drove out. I found Pete pretty quick, but Mike's still missing. Those other two…" He shrugged, pulling one of the plates of lasagna onto his lap. "Wrong place, wrong time. Local kids used the place to party and screw. They picked a bad night."

Say what? "A bad night? They're dead, Grim! And if I hadn't run, it wouldn't have happened!"

He shook his head, glancing up at her stomach's growl. "Eat something, Kitten. You can't think like that," he said, scooping up another mouthful and not meeting her eyes.

"Then please, enlighten me. Tell me how I should think," she spat before tipping back her beer. Her legs crossed, foot bobbing.

Grim glanced at it, tensing. "You feeling responsible for their deaths is what Reaper wants. Trust me, I spent most of my life with the psycho prick. If not that, it would be something worse… it's what he does. He makes you think that if you just fucking obey, it'll stop—but it doesn't, Kit." Grim's knuckles went white around his fork. "Motherfucker'll just laugh, call you a fucking pussy, and pull some shit that makes you wish you'd just killed yourself when you had the chance." He threw his plate onto the tray and raked a hand through his hair.

"What did he do to you?"

Grim snorted, leaning forward with his elbows on his knees, his shaggy blond locks hiding his face. "Bad shit. And I did bad shit to appease him. Shit I knew was wrong… and I probably would have kept doing it, if Clay hadn't gotten me out." He grabbed a beer and cracked it, barking out a hollow laugh. "No, I know I would've kept doing it."

Kit watched him chug half the beer, afraid to ask what she wanted to know.

"Here," he said, tossing his phone on the couch between them. "Call your friend. I gotta get some air." He stood and was out the door before she could draw a breath.

She sat there, staring at the steel slab for a long while before picking up his phone and punching in the code. Her thumb hovered over the apps, then hit phone, abruptly not interested in what else was on there, or why everything was in a weird font.

Chanté answered before the first ring had finished. "Girl? This better be you and not some inbred relation callin' me when I damned well should be out struttin' my stuff and not waitin' on you, like you're important to me or some shit."

"It's me." Kit smiled at her bestie's chiding sass. "That cheap-ass plan you found us doesn't have service up here."

"Please, like it's my fault. Don't tell me that hick town doesn't have a pay phone, and I damn well know you can work a quarter off some poor boy… Look, just tell me you're okay, and then I wanna know all about Grimdarke James. Name like that, he's gotta be fine."

Kit barked out a laugh, then choked on it. James? Grim's last name was James?

Her eyes went to his wallet on the counter.

"Hello, I'm still waiting…"

"How did you—"

"Caller ID, baby girl, now spill."

"Um, yeah, I'm fine… Look, I'm gonna be in the city tomorrow, you around?"

"Am I around? I got a family brunch thing, but then yeah, I'm free."

"Do you? For real? Damn, that's when I'm gonna be there. How much they gonna pay you to show up?" There was no way Chanté was doing anything with her family voluntarily.

"Psh. I wish, and I can't get out of it. This is one of those things where I show up, and they let me go on my merry. If I ghost them, there's hell to pay. And considering my mom's queen bitch, she knows how to make good on that." Chanté's voice didn't leave any doubt she was dead serious, and from the stories Kit had heard, she believed it.

"Damn."

"Ditto." Chanté's voice cracked. "If it was anything else, I'd—"

"Hey, it's no big. Another time." Maybe. If she didn't change. How the hell was she gonna explain that to Chanté? Her view of anything paranormal had mirrored Kit's up until a few hours ago.

She'd lose her.

"So noted. You wearin' your scarf?"

Kit flicked a tear from her cheek. "You know it."

"Good. Promise you'll keep it close. There's some bad mojo floating around… That crazy man hasn't caught up to you, has he?" Silence stretched on the line. "Kit? He did, didn't he? What the fuck happened? Goddamn it, girl, I told you not to go! I could've—"

"I'm fine, but it's… I'm safe now." She glanced at Grim's wallet again. "Look, I'll tell you all about it when we hook up."

"Nuh-uh. You sound all husky like you been cryin' or— Oooh! It's that mystery man, Grimdarke, isn't it? You finally getting some?"

Kit's breath caught—

Chanté squealed. "I knew it! Now spill! He's not your cousin or some shit, right? I mean, not to yuck your yum, if that's your kink. I'm picturing tall dark and handsome… no, that's too Harlequin for you. Redhead with a beard? You know I love me some green eyes and freckles—"

"Stop, stop!" Kit laughed. "His eyes are gray, and that's all you're getting. Shame about that brunch, you could've found out for yourself."

"You're such a bitch… Shit, it's the she-devil herself on the other line. Probably to discuss what she considers appropriate attire for tomorrow. Put a pin in this convo, because we comin' back to it."

"Keep tellin' yourself that." Kit laughed again. "And

you'll be fierce, even in a pants suit. Wear that ugly-ass brooch you bought on 7th."

Chanté gasped. "Don't you dis my flair! I gotta bounce, baby girl, but don't think I'm not Googling your man! Love you!"

"Love you…"

The line went dead, and Kit's eyes went back to Grim's wallet, then flicked to the door.

She was over by the counter before she registered getting up, reaching for the slim leather billfold with its trailing chain. Her fingers smoothed over the embossed club emblem on its face, then flicked it open. Couple hundred in bills, receipt from a burger joint, and a credit card.

His license expired next year, and he didn't look like himself in the photo. Harder, somehow.

Grimdarke M. James

08/13/1991

Shifter/Not eligible for organ donation.

Ten years older than her, and somehow related to Claymore. She tapped the ID against her lips, going back to the couch. What would a Google search bring up?

A shit ton of pics of him with some plastic blonde and articles about Claymore's murder.

Grim was his son.

Kit sipped her beer, thumbing through @463123Nikki_licious's Instagram and trying to process that. Last post was a day ago. She looked thrilled in all of them, and Grim had the same hard edge as his ID, like he was only there because he had to be. She scrolled through the bitch's expansive account, pausing to hit play on a reel taken about a year ago, back at the chapter house bar.

Kit chewed her lip. Yeah, she was totally stalking his ass, but whatever.

The reel began with Grim hunched over his drink, the camera mincing toward him.

"There's my Grimmers!" Goddamn, the bitch's voice could strip the enamel from your teeth.

He shot her a look like he wanted to rip her spine out, and Kit smirked. *Brownie points there, Grimmers.*

"Get that shit outta my face."

"Awww… he's so grumpy! I think my baby boy needs a taste of these…" The camera jostled to a shot of her cleavage. Shit was so fake you could see the saline bags. "Don't you, Grimmers." It wasn't a question and Kit's eyebrow quirked at the ballsy bitch.

The camera was back on him, his expression blank. He growled, and the camera fell to the floor, the reel ending.

In the comments: "You know what happened next… peach, eggplant, squirt, winky face emoji." The replies were all from a bunch of hos congratulating her and telling her to get some, then her gushing back in great detail about how she did.

Vomit.

So he's got a past. It's not like you even knew he existed before the club, and you didn't even want him then. Her fingers tightened around the phone's case.

But she sure as fuck did now.

Something close to a growl tickled up her throat. And right then? Yeah, that was fine with her.

Then you fucking fight to keep him.

Kit tossed the phone down next to Grim's ID and grabbed her plate of cold lasagna. Shit was still delicious.

She was well into her second beer when the door to the hall opened.

Grim came in, his face twisted up and sour like it had been in all those pictures.

CHAPTER NINE

GRIM WHEELED Kit's suitcase into the room, backpack slung over his shoulder, mind about a million miles away. He vaguely registered that Kit was on the couch and had eaten, then he was past her, dropping everything by the bed. He slouched onto its corner, head hanging.

Nikki was blowing shit up.

Way Deuce and Wrench told it, when the crew got back to the clubhouse, mouthing off about Kit in his cut, the crazy bitch had lost it. Burst into those fucking crocodile tears of hers, sobbing about how Grim had done her wrong and alluding to far too much about his past. She'd been desperate to keep him and was so fucking sorry she'd tried to pull rank with Miser's ol' lady.

Yeah, that'd been for the good of the MC, not her Goddamned ego.

And then it'd gotten worse. She spilled that Kit was Reaper's daughter, made up some fucking bullshit about an alliance between him and Grim, then ran off in hysterics, letting everyone draw the wrong fucking conclusions about Clay's murder.

Deuce and Wrench didn't buy it, but apparently, they were in the minority. Nikki's lies went too deep, hit all the right fucking notes—

And MK hadn't said a Goddamned word to the contrary.

—kill—

Yeah, I should've thrown her off that fucking roof when I'd had the chance and sent him down after her.

"Grim?" Kit stood in the doorway. "What happened?"

"The world burned down while I was getting my dick wet," he muttered, then cursed himself. "Sorry, I didn't mean that. There's just… there's an issue back at the club." He sat up to look at her. She was holding his phone and his ID. His stomach lurched at her expression. So much for dick scarf luck rubbing off on him.

"Why do I think that something's named Nikki?"

—whimpering—

He blinked at her. Fuck.

Kit sauntered in and tossed his shit onto the bed. "I told you I was gonna go through it." She put her hands on her hips and cocked one. "Her Insta feed is educational."

Was it? He never looked at that shit. "Yeah?"

"Yeah. Why the fuck were you with her if you can't stand the bitch?"

—?!—

Well, that was not where he'd thought this conversation was gonna go. Grim opened his mouth. Closed it. Opened it again.

Kit ran a hand over his jaw. "Pussycats eat fish, they don't pretend to be one."

And just like that, shit was right.

[EXPOSING BELLY]

Okay, not right, but a shit ton better. He wrapped his arms around Kit's waist, burying his face in her stomach, then staring down at the chippy pink polish on her bare toes. "Because she was blackmailing me. As long as I played along like she was gonna be my queen, she didn't spill about what went down with me and Reaper."

Kit's fingers threaded through his hair. Fuck, that felt

good. "Remind me what that term means again? The MC didn't have a queen when I was a kid."

"It's like..." He blew out a breath, marshaling his thoughts. "Okay, so mollys are random club pussy, ol' ladies are like wives, and queens are another step above that. Doc is Stitch's ol' lady, but the dipshit steps out on her all the time. A queen is a true mate. Not below, equal, and an alpha shares his power with his queen."

Kit's face went still. "And you mean that? About me?"

"Yeah, baby." His thumb traced the bruise on her cheek, and she looked away.

"But you were gonna do that, pretend to be, with Nikki."

Now he couldn't look at her.

—idiot—

Shut the fuck up.

"You gonna tell me why, or do I have to send her a DM to get the skinny?"

—tell her—

What?! You really—

—yes—

"There was this job. Reaper—" Grim's shoulders slumped. "I wouldn't do it, and it pissed him the fuck off. Wasn't the first time. He decided to take me out of the equation. The last couple of years I was with him, he banded me with silver. My cat fucking lost it, went feral and shoved me down so deep I couldn't shift us back..." He chewed on his lip, wishing that was the worst of it.

—tell her—

"Reaper pimped us out," he said in a rush. "He's whacked about genetics, and my lion... Asshole only fed us if we barbed whatever molly he threw into the room. I dunno how many kids I've got out there... I—" His throat closed up, bile rising...

"Shhh... it's done," she murmured holding him tight and

rocking. Grim swallowed raggedly, somehow knowing the anger in her voice wasn't for him. Why wasn't she—

—because she is our mate—

Grim's eyes pinched closed, vision blurry. His fists tightened, gripping the back of her shirt, face pressed tight to her belly. Goddamn, he was so fucking tired of keeping up the front. So fucking sick of—

"Shhh… Let it out, Pussycat. I got you."

And he believed her.

He let go.

She stayed with him, stroking away his pain, letting it soak silently into her shirt. The only person to ever hold him like that. To see. To understand.

His mate… Christ, his queen.

Grim dashed the moisture from his face, then drew her onto his lap, his sigh fluttering her hair. Her breath tickled his throat, waiting, like she knew there was more.

—tell her—

Yeah… Cat was right. He needed to get the rest of it out.

"I dunno how she found out, but a few years ago, out of the blue Nikki waylaid me and spelled out her terms. If Clay found out… it would've killed him. Last night, after his memorial ride, I told her I was done with our deal. He's why I agreed to it." Grim shook his head. "I couldn't let him… I knew this was coming, I just—"

"Didn't know what a vindictive bitch she was gonna be about it?"

He sighed, pinching the bridge of his nose. "No, I was spot on about that, it's the fucking timing. I gotta go to the city tomorrow because there's gonna be a meeting of all the paranormal bigwigs. Clay oversaw the business end of this territory and before Nikki's bullshit, I was his pick to take it over, but the way she's spinning things…" He shook his head, a muscle in his jaw popping.

"Look, I should've told you this sooner, but I didn't know how. Reaper broke into your ma's facility and took her." Kit went rigid, and he plowed ahead, trying to get it all out before she bolted. "Media got footage of him shifting, feds are involved, and the witches are losing their shit. Nikki spilled you're his kid and a bunch of bull about him and me having an alliance. Now the MC's questioning my loyalty and my involvement in Clay's death."

She blew out a long breath. "That all of it?"

"Isn't that enough?"

"Yeah." Kit snuggling back against him, and a purr rumbled in his chest. "But in my experience, there's always another shoe waiting to drop."

The purr cut off as Grim bit his lip. She wasn't wrong, but...

—tell her—

Go the fuck back to sleep. I got this.

—chuffing—

"You do that a lot," Kit said, head tipped to see his face.

"Do what?"

"Fight with yourself."

"You mean my cat."

"Isn't it the same thing?"

"I guess. He is and he isn't. We don't really... whatever. It's hard to explain."

Her eyes narrowed. "Because of what Reaper did?"

"Maybe part of it. We've never really been on the same page." He scrubbed at his face. "Doc calls it disassociation or some shit. Says other shifters are more cohesive with their beasts, like it's harder to tell where one starts and the other begins, have actual conversations. I mainly get bursts of emotion and fragments of thought. We're... I dunno. Independent of each other but not." He looked around the room, not wanting to remember what it took to come back to two legs.

"So what's the other shoe?"

—tell her—

Huh? Oh. "I've told you you're my mate, and I wanna make you my queen… but unless you change, the council won't recognize it, and the MC won't either. Doc says that's why Clay never claimed Marie."

———

Kit's hand went to her throat. "Uber-bitch knew my mother?"

He shrugged. "I guess. I wasn't around back then, and Doc only said something about it after she smelled you on me."

Kit frowned, calculating the likelihood of the woman sharing any stories about her mother. Probably slim, but maybe some of the ol' ladies at the chapter house remembered her, too.

If Claymore hadn't poisoned the pot. "He was your dad."

"Yeah." Grim wasn't looking at her again, picking at the seam of his sweats.

"Then why did Reaper—"

"I never asked, and Clay never told me. Best just to move forward. I know he wasn't your favorite person…" Kit snorted. "… But he saved me. Taught me how to be a man. I owe him so fucking much—"

"And meanwhile he was micromanaging my life and trying to keep me in the same damned box he'd locked my mother in," she muttered, abruptly pissed off about it for reasons she wasn't sure she wanted to examine too closely.

"We'll get her back."

"I'll never get her back, and as far as I'm concerned, she died a long time ago." Kit shrugged, oddly blasé after her initial shock had faded. "I can't say I'm surprised, either. Reaper as much as said he was gonna get her when we were at the house… But she's been non-responsive for over a decade, Grim. Whatever that sick fuck's doing to her body, she's not there for it."

A muscle in his jaw ticked again. "What else did Reaper say?"

"I told you—"

"Yeah, nothing worth hearing, but if I'd known he'd said that, I would've sent a crew out to her facility. We might've been able to stop him."

Her lips pressed flat, feeling like an idiot. "Yeah, okay, you're right, I just—" God, she didn't want to remember, to be in that damned hallway again, but if Grim could tell her about his baggage...

"He said that I looked just like her, but he wasn't inbred enough to fuck me." A growl rumbled through Grim's chest, and she put her hands on his shoulders, steadying them both before continuing. "Said he was gonna go after her... something about Grapple wanting a girl like me, but that he'd already bitten off more than he could chew... Reaper hit me when he smelled you on me, something about not keeping myself pristine, then some shit about skunks and pie, me being useless the way I was and needing to speed up destiny by turning me into catnip. That's when he spit in my mouth."

Thick, tawny fur had sprouted along Grim's nape and she sank her fingers into it. Why did that feel so good...?

"That it?"

"No. Grapple pissing on me was some fucked-up invite to a party. Reaper said you wouldn't be able to refuse, then spouted some Bible crap about a man's responsibility to his kin."

"Of course, he did." Grim's lips curdled, even as his head tipped back, urging her fingers deeper into his ruff. "I am gonna kill him, Kit."

Her heart stuttered, not wanting Grim anywhere near her father or his brothers. "How do you do that? Just make parts of you change. I thought it was all or nothing."

"I dunno, I'm all fucked up. My cat bleeds through sometimes, whether I want him to or not. Damn, that feels good... you talk to your friend while you were stalking me?"

Her lips quirked. "I waited till after, and it was her idea. She's got a thing tomorrow. Can I go to your paranormal bigwig whatsit?"

"Typically no, but considering you're into the middle of this clusterfuck, I'm gonna assume the council will make an exception."

She stopped her scratching and knelt, unzipping her luggage. A charging cable was on top. *Thank you, sweet baby Jesus.* She went to plug in her phone. Didn't work now, but once she got into the city, there were some calls she had to make.

"You're really okay with all this?" Grim asked, like he was pulling a pin from a grenade.

"Kind of have to be, don't I? Nothing I can do about my father or your psycho fuck toy."

He growled. "I never fucked her."

Kit snorted, shaking her head. *Riiight...*

"I didn't. After everything with Reaper..." Grim ran a hand through his hair, sucking on his lip, his pupils waffling again. Kit leaned against the dresser, waiting for it.

"I couldn't get it up, okay? My cat wouldn't let me."

What the—Yeah... not what she was expecting, and it must've shown.

He frowned, staring at his boots. "I mean, I tried, fucked around with her and a couple of other mollys, but... okay, once it worked, but not with her. That wasn't happening. Nikki dosed me with Viagra at a party and my cat flipped the fuck out, went feral, and I ended up back here for six months. She was holding that shit over my head, too. I only messed around with her to keep my man card with the brothers, and her fucking mouth shut."

"Oh come on, don't even try to tell me you weren't hard at the chapter house—"

"My cat's fixated on you, Kit." He stood, gripping her upper arms and skating his thumbs over her flesh. "That means all he sees is you. Nothing else means shit. He's wanted you since that first night in the city. I thought it was just another one of his fucked-up urges, but it's not. I haven't been able to get you out of my damn head. I should've listened to him sooner. This thing between us? It's real, and I'm in fucking deep." His head dipped, and he kissed her, so damn sweet... "You're literally the only one for me. My queen..."

His tongue swept along her lip and she opened, letting him thrust deep, devouring her, the hardness of his body against hers. "Fuck, baby." He took her hand and slid it to the line of rigid flesh tenting his sweats. "This is what you do to me. You. No one else."

———

She ran her hand over him, tracing the curve of his crown to the spreading dampness at its tip, and Grim jerked himself away. "Careful. Lemme get a condom out of my bag. Earlier in the shower was hot as fuck, but it was reckless."

Kit's brow furrowed.

"No, not like I expect us to have sex. I mean, I want to—Christ, I fucking want to—but we shouldn't. Yet, I mean, unless—" He riffled his hair. Damn, this was coming out all wrong and the truth of it just sounded bad, but—"Look, my cat's set on breeding you, and he's enough of an asshole to try if you give him the opportunity. I don't want to force your decision—"

A tear tracked down her cheek, and she looked away.

He froze. Fuck.

—idiot—

You're the fucking reason I have to be an idiot! Shit. "Kit, I-I'm sorry, I didn't—"

"Ugh! Shut up, you idiot—"

—see—

Fuck you!

"—I'm not crying because I'm mad, I'm crying because how can you be so damned good to me? You're perfect..." She threw herself against his chest and hugged him tight.

Him? Perfect?

It took him a second to return the gesture.

Ha! See what now, you fuck? I told you it was a good idea.

—...—

"I'm far from perfect, but I wanna make you happy," he murmured against her hair. "Taking away your choices isn't gonna do that. If I need to wear a bag over my dick, then that's what I'm gonna do—"

"Just... just grab one of the stupid things and kiss me."

Grim dropped to a knee to riffle through his backpack. Where the fuck had—the box was barely in his hands before Kit straddled his thigh, her mouth on his, teasing and nipping. Tongue sliding along the opening of his lips to dip inside. Goddamn, this woman... He palmed the curve of her lower back, her ass, his other hand fisting her hair, feeding on her moans. Sinful and sweet, they only made him hungry for more.

She pulled his tee taut across his shoulders, fingers clenching at the fabric, demanding. Grim rose from the floor, maneuvering her onto the bed, his thigh between her legs. She let out another low moan, hips tipping to rub her core against him. He reached over his shoulder to pull off his tee, then threw it away. Kit's fingers traced over his tats, her mouth hot on his skin. A line of burning desire bloomed in her wake, and his dick throbbed.

"I need to feel you, Kitten." He snapped the waistband of her sweats between kisses. "This shit's gotta go."

"I'll take it off if you put one of those on," she purred, eyeing the box as she stood, slowly pulling up her tee.

Grim's throat bobbed at the slide of cotton giving way to her smooth skin. She paused as the undersides of her breasts were exposed, elbows squeezing them together, the corners of her eyes crinkling above the hem of her tee. Watching him fucking pant for her.

He fisted his cock through his sweats. "Damn. You're killing me. Lemme see," he rasped.

Kit shook her head all coy, looking at the box again.

Shit, yeah, the bag.

He fumbled at the cardboard, tearing out a long streamer of foil-wrapped coins, kicking off his sweats—

Kit's shirt was on the floor, her pants a pile beside it. She pressed a hand to his sternum and plucked the package from his grasp. Her lips dusted over his... "Lie back. I wanna do it."

Grim flopped onto the mattress, throwing his arm over his face with a groan. Her hands slid up his thighs, thumbs ghosting the length of his Adonis belt, following it to his hips, her hair a tickling trail of need over his skin. His cock kicked, weeping desire.

A slick pressure jacketed his crown, rolling down his shaft to settle at the base. His hips thrust, chasing her touch with the slight pinch at his tip, a growl rumbling in his chest—

The warm wetness of her tongue laved over his sac. His hands buried themselves in her hair. Grim moaned as she gently drew one ball into her mouth, her delicate fingers stroking his twitching cock, fighting the urge to throw her down and fuck her like a beast.

—YESSS!—

Shut the fuck—

"Uhhghnnn..." Her lips encircled his tip, and Grim's eyes

rolled back in his head, hips jerking. Kit laughed, the delicious feel of it drawing his balls up. Fuck, if he'd been bare he'd have blown.

"You like that?" she asked, kissing down his length, her eyes dark pools of wickedness.

Was she serious? He quirked his eyebrow, unable to speak, and she laughed again, tongue busy at the base of his cock where the condom didn't cover.

Fuck being bare, he was gonna blow like this.

He sat up, pulling her astride and claiming her mouth with a devouring kiss. Kit's fingers tangled in his hair, pulling just shy of painful, opening for him. Her hips scooted closer, and her pussy so fucking wet against him. She moaned, her head falling back to bare her throat.

Grim's nose swept its length, inhaling the sweetness of her need. His canines elongated, lips peeling back to tease her pulse with their points.

—Bite her!—

No.

But fuck, he wanted to. His hand dipped to her core, tracing her dripping slit before plunging in. Kit gave a soft cry, forehead pressed to his, riding his fingers, breath coming fast, her walls trembling around him, so fucking close...

"You my good girl, baby?" he murmured, kissing her cheek.

"Y-yes..."

He pulled away from her and slapped her pussy.

"Oh!"

"Then you don't come without permission. Hands and knees."

She blinked at him, cheeks flushed, eyes wide, so fucking ready to be defiled. Christ, the filthy shit he was gonna do...

"You gonna make me repeat myself, Kitten?"

She drew in a quick breath and scrambled to the center of the bed, assuming the position.

"Mmm. Thighs wider," he said, kneeling behind her and pressing her shoulder blades down as she complied. "That's it. Arch that ass. I wanna see how wet you are." Goddamn. The insides of her thighs were a mess, lips tumescent and coated with need. He spread them, her little pink hole contracting and spilling cream.

His tongue caught it.

Delving deep and then flattening to lick her clit to asshole, fingers circling her nub. She gasped as he spread her cheeks, flicking across her rosebud.

—WANT—

Yeah… His tongue speared into the tight ring of muscle, soft mewls coming from Kit as she fisted the bedsheets, her thighs quaking beneath his ministrations.

"Ugh, that's so fucking dirty…" she whimpered, pressing back against him for more. "Why does it feel so good?"

Because you were made for me. He pulled a finger full of wetness from her cunt, then eased it into her back hole. His balls drew up tight at the intimate invasion of her body. "You like that?"

"Mmm…oh—" Her asshole tensed around his finger, and she yelped as his hand cracked down on her ass.

"Didn't say you could come," he murmured, rubbing away the blooming pink sting of his hand, room thick with the smell of her arousal. He dribbled a long line of saliva into her pucker, working in another finger, and she arched for more. Fucking hell, this woman…

She whimpered again, hips twitching. "Please, Grim, I-I need you… fuck me."

—YESSS!—

His dick kicked its agreement, and he gripped the base, swallowing hard. He trailed his crown through her sodden folds, fingering her back hole, breath coming too fast, wanting to thrust into her balls-deep, his cat frantic with the need to barb her, to make her his…

Shit. He pulled back. "I can't. I don't trust—"

She huffed out a breath and glared at him over her shoulder, hair a heavenly tangle. "Is he dumb enough to barb me in the ass?"

Wait, she wanted him to—His throat bobbed. "Uhhh… probably not?"

—fuck you—

What? You're pretty fucking stupid.

—growling—

Kit rolled her eyes, settling back down and shimmying her hips. "Let me know when you two figure it out."

—DO IT!—

*I am! Just give me a fucking second, and I swear to Christ, if you fuck this up for me—*Grim ran a hand down his face and cleared his throat. "Just so we're clear, you want my cock in your ass."

She laughed. "Yep."

"Say it." He gave his dick a slow pump, eyes roaming over her dewy flesh. Goddamn. Were they really gonna do this?

Kit peeked back at him over her shoulder. "Fuck my ass, Grim."

Well, that'd be a—Shit. He glanced at the bathroom. "Hold that thought."

She propped her chin up on a hand watching him head in that direction and rummage around under the sink. Nice, it was still here.

"Do I want to know why you've got an industrial-size tub of coconut oil in the bathroom?" she asked with a raised brow as he came back.

Grim spun off the lid, feeling himself flush. "Cat picked up mites the last time he went feral and about scratched himself raw—"

Her nose crinkled. "Eww."

—asshole—

Fuck off. "What can I say? He's a dirty fucker." He smacked her ass and she yelped. "And so am I. Reach back and spread those cheeks for me. Show me where you want it."

Her fingers bit into her skin, flesh dimpling as she parted her backside, still so fucking wet. Her rosebud pulsed as he swept a finger of oil over it, watching it melt against the heat of her skin, seeping down deep.

"Jesus fuck, you've got a sexy asshole," he murmured, lowering himself down, mouth watering, feasting on what she was offering. He worked her clit, sliding into her silken depths and then breaching her pucker. One finger, then two, coaxing long, low moans from her throat. Ass oiled and slick, her breath sped, pleading, hips rocking, inner walls beginning to clench—

He pulled away. "Did I say you could come?"

She let out a frustrated cry. "Please, Grim—"

"Get on your back."

Kit rolled over, hair a fucking mess, knees bent and spread. Her hand rose to tug at her breast, fingers sliding down her stomach—He raised an eyebrow, and she grinned, biting at her thumb. Christ, minx was hot as fuck and knew it.

"Stay just like that." He stroked an oily hand over his cock. "I wanna see your face when I'm inside you."

She bit at her lip, cheeks pinking, the slightest bit of trepidation coloring the lust in her eyes.

"Hey." He lowered himself onto his elbows above her, murmuring against her lips. "We can stop…"

—What?!—

Kit smiled softly and kissed him. "If you don't hurry up and fuck me, I'm gonna beat the shit out of you, Grimdarke James."

—YESSS—

"As my queen commands." He chuckled, notching himself at her back entrance and slowly pushing in. Her fingers tensed on his shoulders, eyes widening with a gasp. His thumb dropped to strum her clit. "Shhh... I promise I'll make it good for you, just relax..."

He inched forward, peppering kisses over her face, groaning as his crown breached her tight ring of muscle. Jesus Fuck... It'd been so Goddamned long... but no way had it ever felt like this...

Kit gasped, brow furrowed, her pebbled nipples pressing against his chest. "Oh, God... I don't—I can't—"

"Shhh... breathe, baby. You're taking my cock so well. Such a good girl. So fucking wet for me..." Honey dripped from her cunt, coating him as he rocked deeper, mouth latching on to her breast, sucking hard.

"Grim!" she cried out, pelvis moving to meet his, nails scoring down his biceps. Her leg slid up his, and he reached down to hook it over his hip.

"That's it. Almost there." Not really, but Goddamn, she was so fucking tight. Grim groaned, his gaze locked with hers. She was so beautiful... pupils blown, cheeks flushed, lips bee-stung from his kisses... He teased them with his. "Take a deep breath," he murmured, waiting to feel her pebbled nipples rise to brush against his chest before burying himself to the hilt with one last push. Kit stifled a surprised shriek, her blunt little teeth biting down on his shoulder—

He froze, aching to do the same.

—YESSS—

Fuuuck... No.

[IRRITATION]

Her lips found his, bringing him back. "I said you could fuck my ass, not that I was into a threesome."

Grim laughed. "Sorry, package deal."

"Mmm." Her hips wiggled. "How about you move that package since it's been delivered?"

"Yeah, you want this?" He drew out long and slow, then

pumped steadily back in. Jesus fuck, had it ever felt this good?

"Yes..." Kit moaned, her back arching, offering up those luscious tits. Goddamn, he needed more hands.

"Play with your pussy, baby. I wanna watch you take my cock." He sat back on his heels, dragging her up his thighs, hands caging her hips. Her fingers dropped to strum over her folds, drawing cream across her clit in quickening circles, pupils blown, head raised to watch his glistening cock disappear between her cheeks, their rhythm speeding with their breath.

Grim licked his lips at her ripening pussy, buried balls-deep and so fucking close...

She dug her shoulders into the bed, pressing his cock deeper, her inner walls tensing and fluttering...

"Oh God, Grim, please let me—"

"Fuck, baby, come with me—"

White light seared across his vision, hot velvet ecstasy milking his cock. He groaned, falling forward and panting, his release pumping through him, into her—Shit, the fucking bag. He should pull out—Kit's legs wrapped around him, hugging him close.

"No... don't go... not yet..." Her body trembled beneath his.

He smoothed back her hair, kissing her forehead. "I don't want to, but I gotta clean up, I'll be right back, okay?"

She sighed but let him go.

Grim slowly pulled out, wincing at the condom's reluctance to leave with his dick.

"It break?"

He glanced up at Kit. She looked less concerned than he would've thought.

—Should've barbed her—

Shut up. "No, it's just really full."

—a waste—

I said shut up.

Kit nodded, hand rising to cover a yawn.

Grim stumbled into the bathroom, cleaning himself up before returning with a warm washcloth. Kit was already half asleep. He gently wiped her down, then hit the light and climbed into bed behind her. She snuggled up close. Damn. He couldn't get over how fucking right she felt in his arms. He kissed the top of her head, and she stirred.

"Are you scared?" she whispered.

"About tomorrow? The moot's gonna suck, but it'll be what it'll be. I'm more scared that when I ask you to ride down on my bike, you'll tell me to fuck off."

She went still, and he started sweating. Shit.

"I've never been on the back of a bike before. Is it hard?"

"Might be, ride's five hours… but if we stop a couple times, it won't be so bad. Deuce is following us in the van, so if it gets to be too much you can ride with him… or just take that, I guess." His stomach soured at the thought. He'd be the laughingstock of the chapter if she didn't want to ride with him after he let her wear his cut, but fuck it. Nikki had already shredded his reputation. How he was gonna come back from that, he had no fucking idea.

"No." Kit blew out a long breath. "I want to try."

His heart leapt. "Yeah?"

She nodded, hugging his arm. "Yeah… What am I supposed to wear to this thing?"

Grim chuckled. "Whatever you want. I'm not doing anything outside the norm, but the witches'll be there like it's a formal event. I'd suggest jeans and something warm. We'll be on the road longer than we're there." *I hope.* "Get some sleep, Kitten. Dawn's gonna come fast."

Minutes ticked by, her breath slowly evened out, and she grew lax in his arms.

Grim stared into the darkness, her damp hair tickling his nose, the smell of *them* heavy in the air. The combo made his dick twitch. So did the way her ass melded against him. His fingers drew lazy circles on the softness of her belly, imagining it rounded beneath his palm. God, she was so fucking soft, so tiny in his arms—

—sleep—

Right. Yeah. Sleep…

Too bad he couldn't take his cat's advice.

CHAPTER TEN

IT WASN'T the first time Kit had awoken in a strange bed, but it was the first time she'd done it while a hot-as-hell, tattooed man in low-slung blue jeans offered her a coffee. He said something and she squinted at him.

"What?" she murmured, blowing a strand of hair from her eyes, looking for a clock. What time was it? 5:30 AM. Was he for real?

Grim chuckled. Who the hell chuckles in the morning? "Come on, baby, up and at 'em. We gotta get on the road. I let you sleep in as long as I could, but the crew's on its way."

She snagged the coffee and glared at him.

"Not a morning person… good to know." He grinned, that frickin' dimple slicing down his clean-shaven cheek. She reached up to touch it, her finger dipping at the whisper of a cleft to his chin.

He kissed her fingertip. "I've been up for a while, got some shit sorted. There's a tray in the other room with breakfast. Get dressed and we can talk."

Kit sat up and sipped her—*blech.*

She must've made a face because Mr. Sunshine chuckled again. She threw a pillow at him, and he backed out of the room with his hands up. "Creamer and sugar are on the tray…"

"Bastard!" she yelled after him. "You can't give someone a

cup of coffee like you're doing them a solid while with-holding everything that makes it drinkable!"

He just laughed from the other room. Fine, he wanted to play? She was gonna fucking play.

Kit clambered out of bed and tore through her suitcase, very conscious of her well-fucked ass as she did her hair and makeup. Not that it was a bad thing. She bit back a smile. Damn, she couldn't wait to tell Chanté. Girl was gonna pass the fuck out, and when she saw Grim? Kit stopped smiling just long enough to apply a coat of vamp red lipstick and wink at herself in the mirror. *Mmm-hmm. That's what I'm talking about.* Let's see who was getting a wake-up call now.

Man was gonna be toast.

She sauntered into the next room to find him lounging on the couch with a cuppa, watching the news.

He turned to her with a smile. "Hey, b—" His jaw dropped and he swore, coffee splashing his lap. He sprang up and brushed at it. "Jesus fuck, Kit…"

"Problem?" she asked, sitting down in front of the break-fast tray. Mmm. Eggs, bacon, and toast. She picked up a triangle to nibble.

His eyes ran over her knee-high brown suede boots, tight jeans, and peasant blouse. She'd been late on rent after Chanté had talked her into buying the latter, but right about now? Totally worth it the way his throat bobbed, ogling the off-the-shoulder neckline and the way her lavender demi bra pushed her breasts up against the semi-sheer ivory fabric.

"N-no. No problem, I just—Damn, woman. You're fucking gorgeous."

She took another slow bite, totally preening. "I thought we were eating on the road."

"We are, this is pre-gaming," he said, adjusting himself before he sat down beside her. "I, uh, got you something."

She glanced at him, trying to act uninterested.

That's it, girl. Make him work for it.

"It's, ah…" He jammed his hand into his pocket and pulled out a chain with a ring. His thumb ran over it, silent for a long moment. "It doesn't feel right having you by my side without something. I can't get you a property patch yet, but I wanted…" Grim looked up at her, his throat bobbing as he swallowed, and what was in his eyes so damned brittle. "Will you wear this?"

He dangled it for her to take.

It was a heavy man's ring with the club emblem. She took it, tracing the gaping maw on its face. Her breath caught. "What does it mean if I do?"

He riffled his hair, glancing away. "That you've got my protection."

"Thought I already had that."

Grim gave a slow nod. "Yeah, but… Shit. It's like a promise, Kit. It's gonna sound crazy, but I told you, my cat's fixated, and fuck if I'm not right there with him. For a shifter, that's… that's it. I can't bite you yet, maybe not ever, but you can damned well wear that ring until I get you one a hell of a lot sparklier."

A lump formed in her throat. It was too soon, too much, too—

Shut the fuck up and take it! You know you want him just as bad!

God help her, she did. However it'd happened, she was head over heels for this man.

Overcome, she just nodded, putting put her back to him. Her eyes closed. How was this real? He swept the tendrils of her updo from her nape. The temperature in the room seemed to tick up, and her breath came fast, and her nipples beaded against the lace of her bra.

"I'm waking you up earlier next time," he murmured, the cool metal of the ring thumping against her breastbone as he latched the clasp. It nestled in her cleavage like it belonged there. His lips tickled over her nape, sharp canines teasing…

"Finish your eggs. The next time you're getting an orgasm for breakfast."

"I'll take one of those now—"

"No time, baby." He chuckled. "The crew's waiting." Grim kissed her cheek and stood. "I'm gonna finish getting ready. Leaving in five, okay?"

Kit nodded, fingering the ring, and dug into breakfast.

A few minutes later, he came out of the bedroom looking every inch a biker. Scuffed shit kickers, jeans and a Henley, leather jacket and his cut. The chain from his wallet winked from below its hem, and a black bandana was around his throat.

The butt of his gun peeked from his jacket as he moved.

"You got your scarf?"

"No, but I can get it," she said, standing.

"Do it. Road dust sucks, and we only got domes." He nodded to a barebones helmet and a pair of goggles on the counter. "Triss is letting you borrow hers."

Kit's eyebrow quirked. "That's gonna fuck up my hair."

"You can always ride in the van."

"No," she said, going into the bedroom for her scarf and her jeans jacket. "I'll deal."

Grim grabbed her arm when she came out and spun her against him. "You are so damn fine, Kit." He palmed her ass and kissed her. "It's gonna be sweet fucking torture having you pressed against my back for five hours."

She smirked. "You can always ride in the van."

He smacked her ass and she squealed. "Not a fucking chance, baby. Come on, crew's waiting."

He took her hand, and Doc let them out, following them up out of the vet's, scowling. Great, she was coming? Sure looked like it. Uber-bitch made for a black van idling in the lot with a brother, presumably Deuce, behind its wheel. Next to it, a dozen riders were waiting for them.

"S'about fucking time," Stitch grumbled.

"Well, that explains it," another said, eye-fucking her.

A low growl came from Grim. "Kit is my mate and queen. You'll respect her as such, or I'll put a fucking bullet in you. We clear?"

Her breath caught at the power in Grim's command, and the crew stepped back as a group, including the Goliath in leather at the end. Damn, that was hot as hell.

"I asked if we were clear!" he barked again.

"Yeah, Grim."

"Shit, man—"

"Crystal."

He gave a curt nod and stalked over to a black-and-chrome monster. Kit fanned herself, chewing on her lip. Man was *fine*…

He threw his leg over his motorcycle and looked back at her, taking his helmet from where it hung off a mirror and strapping it on. "Get on the bike, baby."

Right. The bike. She climbed on behind him, hoping like hell she hadn't somehow done it wrong, pulse thudding in her ears, palms slick. Her fingers fumbled at the helmet's clasp, and he reached around to help her. Her heart skipped at the gesture, and she blinked away the emotion gathering behind her lashes.

"Keep your feet on the pegs and hold onto my waist. Follow my body. I lean, you lean, okay?" he murmured before kissing her quickly and pulling up her scarf so it covered her mouth and nose. "Ready?"

Kit nodded. Grim lifted himself up, then kicked down hard with his right leg.

The motorcycle roared, and she grabbed on to him for dear life with a squeal, feeling him chuckle. He revved it up and peeled out of the parking lot, the rest of the crew trailing behind them.

———

Grim couldn't stop fucking smiling.

The crew had given him shit this morning when he'd first explained things, but the alpha command he'd slapped them upside the head with had sent the message home. He was pretty sure they got it now, if the fist bumps and smirks were any indication.

And he'd need their support. After Doc submitted his intent to pursue the business end of the St. Lawrence territory with the council this morning, the shit that was blowing up his phone… nah. Wasn't gonna worry about it. Shit would fall where it would.

Kit snuggled against his back and Goddamn if he didn't love the feel of her riding bitch. Whatever fuckery Nikki had set him up for, she couldn't take that away.

The weather was perfect, high seventies with a bright blue sky. Kit had done better than he'd expected, pushing through two of the four stops he'd planned on. And now, as they rode through the city, she was totally relaxed against him, like they'd been doing this for years instead of hours. His hand ran over her thigh as they hit another traffic light.

"Where did you say this place was?" she asked over the rumble of his ride.

"Some club called V. It's in the Meat Packing district. There's supposed to be an underground parking—"

"Yeah, I know it. The entrance is off 8th and Jane." She shivered. "That's a vamp club."

The light turned green, and he nodded, accelerating.

Half an hour later they were dipping down the ramp beneath the club into its garage. A big-ass flunky in a gorilla suit with one of those stupid traffic control batons waved them to a cordoned-off section. Grim parked and pulled off his helmet, shaking out his hair.

"Where's the van?" Kit asked, trying to fix hers in one of his mirrors with a frown.

The van was staying outside as insurance if this went bad,

but she didn't need to know that. No way was he gonna do anything to mar that smile she was giving him, despite her quaking thighs from the ride.

"Deuce and Doc are hanging back," he said, climbing off the bike and offering her his hand. She winced, taking it. Damn. Her ass had to be sore… but Jesus, just thinking about last night made him want to bend her over the—

"Mr. James."

Grim turned at the slick voice. "Yeah?"

A witch with a clipboard and wing-tipped shoes stood behind them. The man's pinstriped suit was something straight out of a bad mob movie. "Conrad Styne. Pleasure to meet you. I've been assigned to make sure your party is well taken care of during the moot. And I see you're brought Ms. Parson. I was notified that would be a possibility. I'll update the seating chart accordingly. If you'll follow me, please." He spun on his heel and strode off, not waiting for an answer or the rest of the crew to dismount.

Fucking witches.

"You're gonna have to give us a few, there, Connie," Grim called after him. He could actually see the stick work its way farther up the witch's ass as his spine straightened.

"It's Conrad."

Kit snickered, and Grim put his arm around her shoulders, pulling her close. "Right. How about we wait for the rest of my crew?"

"Of course." The witch's smile was pained. "It's just you're one of the last parties to arrive, and I know you don't want to keep everyone waiting—"

"If we're not the last, then we aren't." Grim's eyes caught the witch's, trapping him like prey.

Conrad's smile went brittle, a bead of sweat tracking down his temple.

"Thanks for waiting." Stitch's hand clapped down on Grim's shoulder breaking their staring contest before one of them did something stupid. "These bones don't move as fast as they used to." He winked, and Kit bit back a smile.

God, she was fucking adorable.

"Yes, well, please, at your leisure, then, sir," the witch said, fumbling with his clipboard.

Stitch took the lead, hobbling over. He repeated his shoulder slapping schtick on Conrad, the witch's knees buckling. "Appreciate it, son. I do appreciate it. Now, tell me all about that agenda you got there."

Grim held back as Stitch monopolized Conrad's attention, his lips close to Kit's ear. "Club's supposed to be neutral, but it won't be. We're in vamp territory, and the witches have them in their pocket. They'll be listening. Eyes open, mouth shut, and take my lead or Stitch's. If Reaper shows, do not react or engage, understand?"

He could tell Kit wasn't happy about it, but she nodded.

Grim kissed her temple. "Stay close. I want you at my side."

"Wait—" She untied the scarf from her throat and stuffed it into the inner breast pocket of his jacket. "I have a feeling you'll need this more than me."

He smirked. "Is dick scarf luck transferable?"

Kit smacked him. "Shut up. Just take it. It—it just makes me feel better knowing you have it, okay?"

"I love you, baby." He ginned at the pleased shock pinking her cheeks and kissed her. "But this is the only dick I'm taking, from you or anyone else."

Her arms threaded around his neck with a Goddamned purr. "You for real?"

"Yeah." Grim palmed her cheek. "I should've said it earlier when I gave you that ring. You're it for me, and my ass is exit only."

She laughed, pushing up on her tiptoes to kiss him. "I'll try to remember that. I-I think I love you too, Grim."

"Then let's do this shit so I can get you home and convince

you." He kissed her again and took her hand, heading the way the crew had gone. The gorilla with the traffic baton glared at them, jerking his head at a steel fire door.

They went through, into a long hall with plush red carpeting and doors branching to bathrooms. Kit paused.

"Can I get a sec to freshen up?" she asked, hand going to her hair. "I knew that helmet was gonna fuck up my 'do."

He palmed the ladies' room door open with a grin. "After you."

Her eyebrow quirked. "You know you can't go in there."

"Yeah, I can."

She laughed, shaking her head, and he stalked in after her with a quick glance down the hall. Shit wouldn't really get going for another hour yet... He ran a hand over his jaw as the door thumped shut behind him and threw the deadbolt. Plenty of time.

Kit looked up from the sink at the clunk, her eyes wide, then traveling down his body.

—want—

That's the plan...

She put her back to the sink, hands gripping the edge of the counter, pupils blowing out as he stepped close. Grim cupped her cheek, thumb dusting over its curve. Damn, he fucking loved how dark her gaze went, every part of her opening up for him.

"You still feel what I did to you last night, Kitten?"

"Yes..."

"Mmm. I thought about it the whole ride down. My cock sliding in and out of that tight little asshole. Next time I'm gonna bend you over and take it hard." His dick pressed against his jeans, voice thick and syrupy with need. "I wanna hear you scream when I fuck you. You wanna scream for me, baby?" Her eyes dropped to his lips, her own parting with a little nod. He teased them, nipping at their pillowy softness, his tongue darting to lick along their seam.

"You did so good riding down… You want your reward?"

"Yes…" she moaned, and a chuckle rumbled in his chest.

"Then you gotta be quiet. The vamps in the next room already know we're in here." His mouth dipped, laving a long line from her collarbone to the divot behind her ear. "They can hear your heartbeat speeding up." His fingers released the buttons of her blouse, pushing it aside, hands cupping her breast through that sexy-as-hell bra. "Your moans…" The scent of her arousal swirled in the air. She bit back a cry as he pushed the cups down, her taut nipples begging for his mouth.

Her fingers threaded through his hair as he knelt, lips capturing a rosy bud and sucking. "Ah… sweet baby Jesus, Grim… what you do to me…"

"Nah…" He kneaded her sweet flesh, mouth on the other side, fingers tugging the slippery peak he'd just left. "It's what I'm gonna do. Now, keep quiet and take what I give you."

He raised her foot to his thigh, eyes filled with dark promise as he pulled the zipper down to remove her boot. A flush spread across her chest, and she glanced at the door. Grim smiled and popped the button on her jeans, working them over her hips.

"Goddamn." Her panties matched the bra, a lacy lavender bit of not-much-there. Saliva filled his mouth, his canines extending.

"You ruin these, and I'll—"

She gasped as he flicked out a claw and they fluttered down around her ankle.

"Whoops…"

"Those were La Perla, you asshole!"

Grim shrugged. "They were in my way." His hands were on her hips, lifting her thigh over his shoulder, nose buried in her mound, inhaling—motherfucker, she smelled so Goddamned decadent—tongue tracing her slit—

—Feast—

Her head tipped back, hands at his ears. Bitten-back moans, breaths heavy and stuttered. He parted her folds, lapping cream and drawing it up and around her clit. Sucking her into his mouth and flicking. She trembled, thighs shaking, going rigid as his fingers slid into her molten core. His dick wept for her, balls aching, wanting to be so fucking deep—

"Oh God, Grim… Please…" Kit's walls fluttered and danced around his fingers.

"Come for me, baby. Gimme that honey…"

She bit back another cry, her nails digging into his scalp, delicious half-moons of pain, hips tilting to grind against him—

Her breath hitched and she went liquid, body undulating, seeking his, head thrown back, heel riding up his shoulder blade, pussy milking his fingers. Goddamn, she was a fucking goddess when she came. Grim moaned, gorging himself on her release, worshiping her offering.

Her tremors slowly subsided, and he slid up her body to kiss her, feeding her back her desire, his, a torturous ache. Her hands dropped to his belt buckle, his cock bucking in anticipation. Fuck. As much as he wanted her fingers wrapped around him…

"Let me do it, baby, I'm a fucking mess," he murmured against her lips, freeing his sticky shaft from its prison. His hand stroked over his aching length, groaning as Kit sucked his tongue into her mouth. Goddamn, this wasn't gonna take long… Panting, he broke their kiss. "I wanna come on your tits. Play with them for me." The entire ride down they'd been sweet insanity pressed against him.

Kit scooted against the mirror, one leg bent, her swollen clit peeking from damp curls, the air laden with citrus, cinnamon, and sin. She arched her back, palms smoothing over her breasts, pressing them together, then pinching her nipples taut on the retreat, her breath catching. Eyes bright, cheeks flushed—

"Like this?"

"Yeah," he ground out through clenched teeth, his fist pumping over his dick and down again, balls clenching—" You're so fucking beautif—ah—" Light flared across his vision, exploding hues of lust. Thick cords of ecstasy shot from his crown, lines of heated desire branding her chest.

She rubbed his release over her breasts, head back, lips parted. "Oh God, yes, mark me, baby, make me yours…"

"You are mine." He pulled her close by her nape, his kiss fierce, then tender. The contentment of the afterglow settling in. "My queen."

Kit smiled, then concern washed over her delicate features. "Wait, they're really all going to know what we did—"

Grim laughed, a grin stretching across his face. "Every fucking one of them."

She smacked him, pushing off the counter and pulling her jeans back on. "I can't believe you ruined my panties. You know how expensive those were?"

He shoved them into his pocket. "I'll buy you as many pairs as you want."

"You will, huh?" Her eyebrow quirked, reaching for the paper towels.

"No." He caged her wrist, arms sliding around her, gaze capturing hers in the mirror as he slicked the last remnants of his seed into her skin. "Leave it. I want you to go out there with me all over you."

"That's filthy," she murmured, blushing but not sounding opposed.

He nipped at her ear. "Be my good girl and do as you're told."

"Mmm. Since you asked so nice, Pussycat."

His dick twitched at the smirk in her voice, and he

slapped her ass, stepping back. "Finish freshening up, baby. We got an entrance to make."

Kit's cheeks pinked as she fixed her hair and makeup, then turned with a sigh.

"Ready?" he asked.

"Nope, but let's go."

They exited the bathroom and followed the hall to a cavernous club space, lit up bright by the house lights. At the far end of the room, a long table with flowers was set up on a dais. Circular tables with centerpieces dotted the rest of the space. Christ, it was like they were at some fucked-up wedding reception, and the place was milling with people taking advantage of a swanky buffet.

Didn't stop them from eyeing him and Kit as soon as they stepped into the room, and Grim didn't bother to stop the smirk on his face from blooming into a full-blown grin. He nodded to the shifters in cuts he recognized, way too fucking pleased by their flaring nostrils and raised brows.

Kit burrowed closer under his arm, her cheeks crimson. "I didn't know there were going to be so many people…"

"Yeah, looks like the entire region and surrounding territories showed up." Considering the shit going down, that shouldn't be unexpected. Roughly a third of them were allies. The rest were neutral, or had been when Clay was alive. By some of the angry stares he was getting, that'd changed.

Nikki had been very, very busy.

Witches stood in isolated pockets twirling the stems of their champagne flutes, easily recognizable in their ostentatious finery and how they looked down their noses at everyone else.

The vamps stayed to the shadows, watching the crowd like they were picking out their next meal. Of all the paranormals, they were the most low-key, but sick fucks when it came to playing with humans, and their ability to compel was no joke. More than a few were far too interested in Kit, and Grim preemptively shoved down his cat.

You cannot lose your shit here. You'll get her killed.
[SUBMISSION]
Grim froze mid-step, just about swallowing his teeth.
What?!
—you are alpha here. protect our queen—
Are you fucking with me?

Kit shot him a look, her brow furrowed. He took her hand, kissing her knuckles and leading her through the crowd. Whispers swirled in their wake, and the space between Grim's shoulder blades prickled. Above the main floor were two levels of balconies, deep in shadow, and the table they'd been assigned was close to the middle of the room. Stitch sprawled out in a chair smoking his vape, and the MC's enforcer, Brick, was working through what looked like his fourth plate from the buffet. The rest of the crew warily eyed the crowd, pieces loose in their holsters. They were well-aware that they were sitting ducks if someone opened fire from up above.

Grim caught Wrench's eye, then flicked his gaze to the balcony. The man nodded, tapping another one of their crew. They melted into the crowd to check it out—

"Kit?" Grim froze at the deep baritone. She turned. "It is you! Whatever are you doing here? Are you back from your holiday? Cecelia will be delighted!" A vamp was abruptly in front of her, hands on her shoulders, air kissing both her cheeks—And completely fucking ignoring the death stare Grim was giving him.

A warning growl rumbled in his throat.

—trust our queen—
Oh, I trust her, but this fucker—

Kit squeezed Grim's hand. "Hi, Mr. Asorav," she said, giving the silver-haired vamp in head-to-toe Armani a smile and a little wave like they were old friends. "I was gonna call you about that…"

She trailed off when the vamp didn't return her smile. His eyes narrowed, and a long-nailed finger skated over her bruised cheek, a decided chill emanating from him. "Who did this to you?"

The crowd around them edged away.

Kit blushed. "It's nothing—"

"Who. Damaged. You?" The vamp's breath hissed out, frosting her eyelashes. His head moved in a painfully slow arc to glare at Grim. "Did you do this, *cat*?"

Grim's smile wasn't pleasant. Was Asorav trying to pick a fight?

—be nice—

What? Who the hell are you today?

—he protects our queen—

"No, Mr. Asorav, it was Reaper," Kit said, stepping between them. "Grim's been taking care of me."

Asorav didn't blink. "Is that so?"

She put a hand on his arm. "It is. Mr. Asorav, please."

"Mmm." The temperature rose to normal, and the vamp straightened his suit jacket. His eyes skated over her, pausing at the ring nestled between her tits, then zeroing in on her hand in Grim's, his cheeks sucking in.

That's right motherfucker, she's mine.

The vamp's lip twitched like he'd heard him. "If it is your wish that he be spared…"

The blood drained from Grim's face. The fuck?! Was he seriously discussing kill-rights with her?

—told you to be nice—

Fuck off, like you knew.

Kit rolled her eyes. "He's only ever been wonderful to me, so yes. I wish him spared."

"Indeed. Then it shall be so for as long as you deem him worthy."

Holy shit, he was, and she had no fucking idea. Grim's throat bobbed, and the son of a bitch smirked at him.

"Well, now that that's settled, I'll let you get to your seats, I believe we're beginning shortly. It was good to see you. And Kit, should you have reason to stay in the city longer than anticipated, do drop by, any time. I've plenty of rooms. Mr. James and his men are also welcome whilst in your company. Cecelia will be devastated if you don't visit."

"Sure, Mr. Asorav, I'll try to do that."

Grim ran a hand down his face. Christ, she said it like she meant it…

The vamp's flinty eyes met Grim's. "Do."

The fuck was that about? He turned to Kit as Asorav went to scare the shit out of someone else. "Who the hell is Cecelia and how the fuck do you know the Darkling?"

"I don't know anything about a darkling, but Cecelia's Mr. Asorav's Teacup Pomeranian. I walk her in the afternoons." Kit laughed. "What? She's sweet."

"Not a darkling, the Darkling. He's the vampire queen's fucking hitman." Grim ran his hand down his face. "And you walk his dog."

"Yeah, his and a couple other vamps'." She shrugged. "It's easy money."

Easy—fuck. Grim didn't have the bandwidth to deal with her being a dog walker to the undead. Especially not *that* undead.

"Come on, let's sit."

He pulled out her chair and flicked away the stupid folded cards assigning seats. His phone pinged, and he glanced at it.

Wrench had sent a text. *Snipers.*

Yeah, that sounded about right. *Leave them,* he sent back, refraining from looking at the balcony as he sat and glad he'd put Kit next to Brick. If it came down to it, the brother was big enough to shield her from fire coming in three simultaneous directions. Around them, the rest of the room was settling in.

"You got business with the Darkling?" Stitch asked, fiddling with his vape.

"Nope. Apparently, his dog misses Kit."

The sound system clicked on, and a microphone thumped. Stitch's mouth opened, and a voice like melted chocolate came over the speakers, cutting off whatever he was about to say.

"If you all can take your seats again, we'll move on to the next bit of business." At the long table at the end of the room, Sama, the leader of the region's coven of witches, and self-appointed queen of their sect, stood resplendent in a gold silk sari. The six chairs to either side of her had been claimed by Asorav and the rest of the council.

Behind her stood a triad of witches, all clearly related by their features and dress. The man in the center, flanked by women so much shorter it was comical, pulled at the neck of his kurta. Dude looked like he'd rather be chewing glass than standing up there.

Grim could relate.

Kit's hand squeezed his thigh, her eyes huge as they met his.

"That's Chanté!"

———

No joke. Her bestie was a fucking witch, and by the looks of it, the frickin' witch queen, Sama herself, was Chanté's mom. The mini-bitches to either side had to be her sisters, Labha and Kameli.

Woman was a hell of a lot cunt-ier in person than her TV spots had led Kit to believe. She fell back in her chair. Whatever was coming out of Sama's mouth as she addressed the room didn't register. Damn, Chanté was paranormal royalty… Little snippets of what Kit's bestie had dropped about her family abruptly clicked into place, and Kit couldn't even be mad. Wasn't like she'd spilled the full skinny on her fucked-up family, either.

"Which one?" Grim murmured, scooting his chair closer.

"Tall one in the back." And damned if she didn't look miserable up there, fidgeting like someone had poured her into the wrong skin. How could her family be so fucking callous to make her stand up there like that?

"Wait, *him*?"

"Don't." She shot Grim a look, and he just shook his head, settling in his seat with his arm draped over the back of her chair. Well, that attitude was gonna have to change. Kit pulled out her phone, all kinds of pissed. The damned thing blew up as soon as it powered on.

She ignored all of it, going to Chanté's thread and texting her. *wtf? ur mom didn't want u takin the spotlight? Fuck her. U still prettiest up there*

Her bestie's hand drifted to her pocket, and she glanced down, a smile flitting across her face a half-second before turning to sheer panic. Her eyes snapped up, scanning the room and landing on Kit's.

She raised a brow. *Mmm-hmm. You got some explaining to do.*

Chanté's Adam's apple bobbed. She glanced at her mom, then pulled her phone again. One of the mini-bitches rolled her eyes and elbowed her to put it away.

Kit's phone buzzed. *nm me. E!!! robert paco!!!*

She stared at Chanté's text. For real? She could see how this could be an emergency, but the Robert Paco clusterfuck had entailed a stolen—sorry, liberated—Prada purse Chanté had to fucking have, and them acting like they didn't know each other to get out of it without getting shot.

The potential parallels to their current situation, minus the purse, didn't escape Kit.

Neither did the fact that not getting shot did not mean they hadn't been shot *at*.

Chanté's big brown eyes were pleading. Kit sighed, and she nodded. Her bestie slumped with relief, then made a gesture at her throat. What? Her scarf? She wanted to know about that now? Kit gave her head a little shake and tipped her head with a glance at Grim.

Woman looked like she was gonna pass out.

What the hell was going on?

"… the abduction of Marie Cezniof—"

Kit's attention snapped to the witch queen at the mention of her mother's name.

"—has far reaching implications for the paranormal community as a whole. Already, the media has spun the incident as a public safety issue, and with the recent spate of murders related to St. Laurence County, the council can't disagree."

"So kill the fucker and have done," someone called out from across the room.

Sama's lips tightened. "Your suggestion has been noted, Mr. Billings, but it's too late for that. It is the council's ruling that Reaper Ells be brought in for trial."

The room erupted in protest and light burst from her palm with a deafening bang.

"Enough! The human population must see that we can police our own in accordance with their version of civilized justice. As of twelve hours ago, the Blēda have been dispatched to bring him and any accomplices in." Her gaze fell on Grim and Kit broke out in a cold sweat.

"We appreciate Mr. James coming in voluntarily."

Wait, what? Furious whispering swirled through the room.

"Why wouldn't I?" Grim replied, man-spreading in his chair like he didn't have a care in the world.

Wait, that asshole knew this was gonna happen? Kit's teeth ground together. He was a fucking dead man.

"I got nothing to hide," he said, arms flinging wide, "and not a damned thing to do with any of it."

Sama's lips pursed into a condescending moue. "Certain sources dispute that claim, and with the evidence already given, I very much doubt that, Mr. James, but since the media has not named you specifically, the council has determined that your submittal to an oculus will suffice to prove your innocence or guilt." Her smile was cold, and Grim tensed, the room churning with shocked murmurs.

An oculus? What the hell were they talking about?

"If you aren't willing to submit, I'm afraid we'll have to take you into custody until your involvement in this matter can be determined." She said it like she already knew he wouldn't and was fucking tickled about it. Damn, Chanté's mom really was an evil bitch, and whatever she was laying down had Grim's crew tensing up and going for their guns.

A red dot appeared on one of the brothers' chests, and Kit's eyes went to the balcony. Sweet baby Jesus, there were snipers...

Grim sat forward and licked across his teeth. "And who would be the 'impartial judge' performing the spell?"

Chanté stepped forward, shoving one of her sisters back so hard she stumbled.

"I will."

CHAPTER ELEVEN

GRIM COULDN'T HELP but note the rapid succession of surprise, pride, and then suspicion that flicked across Sama's face as Chanté—seriously, that was fucking Chanté?—stepped forward. The Witch Queen opened her mouth like she was about to put a kibosh on the offer and that settled it.

"I accept the terms given for the oculus," he called out.

The entire room went silent, looking at him like he'd lost his mind.

Shit, maybe he had.

Sama's expression went hard. As much as she hadn't expected Chanté to step up, she really hadn't expected Grim to agree to it.

Yeah. Nobody had, and there was a reason for that.

Forget about that fact that a fucking witch was going to be digging around in his head and the process was supposed to fuck you up royally afterward, shifters had a thing about submitting. To a stronger alpha, yeah, status quo. To anyone else? Hell no. And if that someone was a witch?

That'd be a hell fucking no, followed by manic laughter for even suggesting it.

Shit. With all the history Clay had poured down his throat, Grim didn't think it'd ever been done.

Not voluntarily at least.

But given the choice between an oculus being witnessed by the entire council or him being whisked off some place where he could conveniently disappear, leaving Kit unprotected?

—suck it up—

Yeah. That about covers it.

"Splendid," Sama said, her tone conveying that it was anything but. "A room has been prepared. Shall we? I think we'd all like to go about our day." She flashed a fake-as-hell smile at the room, then grabbed Chanté's sleeve as she swept past, pulling Kit's bestie in her wake.

"What is going on? What's an oculus?" Kit hissed at Grim, the crowd around them shrinking back like he had something communicable, the air thick with their murmuring.

Yep, he was fucking stupid.

Or maybe he was feeling lucky. He did have a dick scarf.

Grim scrubbed at his face. "It's a spell where they can see into your head, like a window."

"Yeah," Stitch growled. "Problem is, there ain't no limits on it. Our boy here's just agreed to let them poke into whatever the fuck they want and hope to hell they report it accurately—"

"And don't leave any directives behind," Wrench muttered. "Wouldn't fucking bet on it considering how eager that poof was to get his hands on you. Don't worry, Grim, I'll take care of your girl while you're catchin' for the other team."

"How about I kick your backward hillbilly ass for labeling people like that instead?" Kit fired back, smoke practically coming out of her ears.

—laughter—

"Yeah, stop being an asshole," Grim muttered. That shit wasn't cool, but them fucking around in his head was a definite possibility… He took Kit's hand, dragging her glare from Wrench. "You trust her?"

"Chanté? Yeah. She's… yeah." Her shoulders slumped and she chewed her lip, brow etched with concern. "The last time she had a family thing and they deadnamed her, she didn't leave her apartment for weeks. Her being up there in front of all these people like that… This is gonna fuck with her hard. I gotta make sure she's okay. Do you think we can—"

"Mr. James?" Conrad was back. "If you'll follow me, please. Ms. Parson's presence has also been requested."

Grim kept his gaze on Kit, ignoring the pompous fuck waiting on him. Damn, she was really upset, and this was gonna take him out of the game for God only knew how long… shit, what if she changed without him?

—whimpering—

There was nothing fucking for it. He pulled her close, kissing her forehead. "Stitch. You and the crew, get her whatever she needs."

The old man tipped an imaginary cap at him, and the rest gave him solemn nods.

Kit's eyes flew between them. "Wait, what—"

"I get two witnesses, right?" Grim asked the witch.

"Correct…" He didn't sound real thrilled with Grim's grasp on protocol. Fuck him and all this shit. Clay hadn't trusted witches enough to hold his beer and had made certain Grim could hold his own. "If Kit's one, Stitch is my second."

Conrad's mouth soured, but he nodded. "Follow me, please."

The crowd went silent, parting as they passed, a clamorous din crashing in their wake. Kit's palm, slick with sweat, found his and he squeezed it.

"I don't understand, why do you want the crew to—"

"Because this is gonna fuck me up. No, baby, I'll be fine," he amended at her anxious gasp, hoping to hell it was true. "Just out of it for a while. I need you to pay attention. There'll be a list of questions. We get to look them over beforehand.

They're not supposed to ask anything outside of what's agreed upon. They can ask for detail or clarification, but you and Stitch are there to make sure they don't go outside the scope that's been set."

She swallowed, trembling against him. "And if they do?"

He grimaced. "Technically, it can't be held against me, but that's horseshit, and I won't remember any of it."

She nodded and they stepped into the room.

It was empty save for a narrow straight-backed chair, the council, Sama, and her brood. Those last four were whispering furiously in the far corner. The rest of the council stood on the other side of the room, deep in their own murmured discussion.

—*listen*—

Grim's hearing shifted to his cat's, and the witches' voices sharpened.

"…pardon me if your sudden participation seems curious, Cabir."

Damn. That's what Kit must've meant about deadnaming. By Chanté's expression, that shit cut deep.

"I don't see why. Haven't you been up my—" Chanté broke off at her mother's glare. "—Sorry, *requested* I take more interest in family affairs?"

"He just wants to find a memory of that man jacking off," one of the girls snarked.

Sama's hand snaked out and slapped her. "Mind your tongue."

"Apologies, Mā." Her face said something different, but Sama was too busy dressing down Chanté to notice.

"We have obligations, and you know your duty."

Chanté bowed her head, and the witch queen sniffed, apparently still not satisfied.

"It's done, Mā." the other girl said. "The shifter accepted."

"Yes." Sama drew out the S like a serpent, eyeing Chanté.

"And wasn't that just as unexpected? Let's find out why." She swept into the center of the room and clapped her hands. The council's discussion broke off, and they dispersed around the perimeter in a large circle.

Stitch handed Grim a document. "Here it is. You okay with all this?"

Grim didn't bother looking at it. "Are you?"

"Nope, but it's still happenin'. Nikki's bullshit has legs."

"Figured. S'how rumors work." Grim kissed Kit's brow. "Stay with Stitch."

Kit bit her lip with a little nod, keeping quiet. She hadn't so much as looked in Chanté's direction since they'd come in.

Sama drew a jagged pair of crystals from the folds of her sari as Grim approached. He stood to one side of her, and Chanté took her place on the other. "The oculus begins with the verification of impartiality," Sama intoned. "Hands."

Grim's jaw clenched at the curt directive, but he echoed Chanté, extending his palm to parallel hers. Sama was issuing commands on purpose to get under his skin. He wasn't doing this for her, he was doing it for Kit. If he got locked up, she was as good as Reaper's.

The witch placed a crystal in each of their palms, a line of fire zinging up Grim's arm on contact, like he'd cracked his elbow on something, his fingers going numb. Fuck, that hurt…

After a breath, the sensation subsided to a dull throb, and Sama gave a satisfied hum, watching the glittering shards go from milky to translucent.

"They will remain clear if all answers given are true. Do you, Grimdarke James, submit to the oculus of your own free will?"

"Yeah." Technically he'd rather be giving Stitch a pedicure, but yes, he'd raised his hand for this clusterfuck. The crystal agreed, staying clear.

"And have either of you had any prior dealings that could call the impartiality of your viewing into question?"

They both answered in the negative.

She turned to Chanté. "Then why have you volunteered to administer the test in Labha's place?"

From Chanté's expression, that was not part of the standardized questions. She licked her lips and they twitched, her jaw going stubborn. "Kameli was right. I want to see his dick."

———

Kit clapped a hand over her mouth trying not to laugh. Fucking Chanté. The reactions from council ringing the trio ranged from sucking in horrified gasps to snickers, and Grim's shoulders shook, like he was trying not to laugh. Her bestie flicked away a non-existent lock from her cheek, smug as fuck.

Her mother wasn't havin' it. Her nostrils flared, and she snatched the crystals from their hands. "You," she barked at Grim. "Chair, now."

He froze, his pupils waffling, and the amusement draining from his face. Slowly, he lowered himself down onto the straight-backed seat, more suited to an anemic granny than his six-foot-plus frame. It looked like he was trying to squeeze into a kindergartener's desk chair.

Chanté shook her hands out and took her place behind him, widening her stance before resting her fingertips on his temples.

"Proceed," Sama snapped, not even trying to pretend she wasn't a bitch.

A glow surrounded Chanté's hands and she frowned. Grim's skin went waxy and pale, his pupils waffling again. Sama's head cocked, noticing the fluctuation with far too much interest.

His lids dropped.

The expression of intense concentration Chanté had been rocking slid off her face as Grim went slack. Kit's nails dug into her palms and Stitch put his hand on her shoulder, his brows knitted.

"Ask," Chanté's voice rasped out.

Sama picked up the document of questions like it was a particularly delicious toffee. Her brow arched, and Kit's furrowed. Why hadn't Grim bothered to read it?

"Do you see anything that corroborates the allegations of Grimdarke James's involvement with Reaper Ells?" Sama asked.

A frown marred Chanté's forehead. "Clarify."

Her mother huffed. "Did Grimdarke James have anything to do with the abduction of Marie Cezniof?"

"No. There are no memories related to this."

"Did Grimdarke James have any involvement with the murder of Claymore James?"

Grim's body spasmed, his shirt darkening with sweat. A low moan scraped from his throat.

"He witnessed his death, but no. It shocked and devastated him."

The council murmured around them, and Sama wasn't pleased with the additional detail.

"Have Grimdarke James and Reaper Ells had contact since that night?" she gritted out.

"Yes, but not directly."

Grim's head jerked back, jaw clenching, the cords in his throat in rictus.

"Expound." The woman was abruptly salivating.

A tear ran from beneath Chanté's lashes. "Threats against Grimdarke's loved ones have been made. I see no basis for their issuance, and he has not retaliated."

"Why not?"

"Because he's genuinely a good man and is trying to let the council do its job."

The head witch's teeth ground together, not pleased by that tidbit either.

"Next question, Sama," Mr. Asorav said from behind her, with a nod at Kit. She took a steadying breath. He and Grim didn't seem to like each other, but Mr. Asorav had always been kind to her, and she was glad she had a friend in the room.

Sama flicked the document. "Is Grimdarke James working with Reaper Ells in any capacity?"

"No. He hates the motherfucker and wants him dead."

Make that two friends. Kit wasn't sure what Chanté's deal as a witch was, but she didn't doubt her bestie had her back.

"I think we're done here," a white-haired woman bit out in a dry English accent. "Please conclude the oculus."

"One last question…" Sama's gaze fell on Kit. "Is there any truth to the accusation that Grimdarke James intends on making Reaper Ells' half-breed daughter his queen?"

"That ain't on the list!" Stitch snarled, stepping in front of her.

Several in the council broke their silence:

"Really, Sama—"

"I was curious about that too…"

Grim's body was still, his brow smooth.

"No." Chanté's voice was decisive. "He has no plans to make her his queen."

Wait, he didn't? But he'd said… Kit bit her lip, trying to kill the hurt in her chest.

"Well. I suppose that's it, then. As I suspected, just another one of his paramours. Conclude." Sama smirked. The fuck? Had Sama asked that just to mess with her? God, the way she treated Chanté was straight-up fucking wrong, but that was a Goddamned cherry on the sanctimonious cunt's sundae. Did she get off on hurting people?

The glow from Chanté's hands snuffed out, and she dropped them from Grim's temples. He slumped bonelessly in the chair. Her bestie didn't look much better.

"And now we've some questions for you, Ms. Parson," the bitch said, her expression making it clear she was totally getting off on the anguish she'd just caused.

Yeah, answering questions was the last thing Kit wanted to do. She glanced at Grim. "For me? But—"

"I got him." Stitch patted her shoulder and went to kneel before Grim, lightly slapping at his face to wake him.

Sama smiled, and it wasn't comforting in the slightest. "Yes. Questions. You've a very interesting past. Reaper Ells' daughter, raised by Claymore James—"

"My mother and my aunt raised me. The other two just repeatedly fucked up my life."

Sama snorted. "Is that why you went back to the scene of the crime?"

"If you're talking about my mother being shot, I went back to Flatts because Reaper was stalking me, and Claymore had said that the MC would give me sanctuary."

"That strikes me as odd, considering any fool can see you being there would start a war."

"Then I'm a fool, because I don't know jack shit about any of that."

"Hmm. Yet you worked at the club Claymore was executed in…" Sama cocked a brow as if she'd tripped Kit up with some major revelation.

She laughed, so fucking done with this bitch. "Lady, I hated Claymore, but I didn't have shit to do with his death, and if I had to pick, it would've been Reaper with half his face blown off that night. Claymore was a controlling prick, but my father's a straight-up monster who's most likely fucking the unresponsive shell he turned my mother into. Tell me again why I'd hang with him?" The Witch Queen's face was livid, but she had shit to say to that. "Yeah, I thought so. We done here?"

"Yes, I think we've heard just about enough of that, thank you," the white-haired woman snapped.

"And the council's ruling?" Stitch ground out.

Kit's breath caught, the man was fucking pissed. He muttered something, sending a text with one hand and steadying Grim with the other. Poor guy had fallen forward, his hands gripping his temples like he was trying to hold his head together.

Mr. Asorav cleared his throat. "Several parties in the main room have asked to speak before we make a decision, and, in light of Mr. James's testimony, further discussion amongst the council must take place regarding the evidence we received." His eyes flicked to Sama and another man in the room. "I'm assuming that will take a fair amount of time. I suggest you find someplace close to await the outcome."

Kit's brow furrowed at the pointed look he gave her during that last bit. *Hold up…*

Grim groaned as Stitch helped him out of the chair, throwing his arm over his shoulder and falling against the old man. "That fucking sucked. Hope my dick was worth it."

"I don't kiss and tell," Chanté teased half-heartedly, taking a bottle of water from one of her sisters. The girl laughed.

Sama looked like she was chewing nails, and they were red fucking hot.

"We can't leave?" Kit asked, pressing up under the arm Grim didn't have around Stitch. He sagged between them, groaning.

"No," Stitch growled. "If he leaves the district before they clear him of charges, they'll get him for contempt, and it'll taint their ruling. We need to find someplace to hole up. Fucking safe house is on the other side of the city…"

Kit glanced back at Mr. Asorav, and he gave a subtle nod.

Well, this was gonna go over like broccoli for breakfast. "I got a place, and it's close."

"It secure?"

She bit her lip, thinking about the vamp's penthouse with its thick, amber-tinted windows. "Yeah, I don't have my swipe card, but I can still get us in." Kit glanced at Mr. Asorav again, but he was deep in discussion with the white-haired lady.

Conflict warred in Stitch's eyes.

"Do it..." Grim's head lolled. He coughed, and a wet splat of vomit hit the floor.

Stitch swore. "Fine. Shit goes sideways, it's on you. Brick's on his way back, and the rest of the crew's meeting us out front," he muttered. "We gotta get him to Doc..."

"Brick?"

"Yeah, big guy you were sitting next to." Stitch grimaced, hefting Grim through the door. "I ain't carrying his ass outside and neither are you."

Between the two of them, they manhandled Grim into the corridor. The door slammed behind them, and he flinched at the noise, going green.

"Ain't never seen Sama with a stick quite so far up her ass," Stitch said. "Them witches... some shit ain't right."

"Gonna puke—" Grim collapsed to his knees, retching.

Both breakfasts and probably a dinner or two came up. Kit held his hair, gaining a new appreciation for the gesture.

Stitch kept talking to himself as if nothing was happening. "Figured something was awry with them snipers, and if the witches is leanin' on the vamps to commit fuckery again..." He shook his head, hefting Grim upright when he'd stopped heaving.

Grim moaned, wiping his sleeve across his mouth. "Fuck, it's bright... they stick to the questions?"

"Bitch asked if you intended to make Kit your queen."

She concentrated on the floor, not wanting either of them to see the tears in her eyes.

"And?" Grim leaned his head against the wall, his face drawn and streaked with sweat. He swept a hand over his forehead. "Fuck, this hurts... why you way over there, Kitten?"

She shook her head, her arms crossed over her stomach.

His brow scrunched up. "What's wrong?"

"What's wrong?" Stitch snorted, backing up as Brick lumbered around the corner. "For all your posturing earlier on the subject, that witch said you're not." He raised a grizzled brow and pulled out his vape.

A smile played over Grim's lips. "S'cause she already is my queen." His eyes met Kit's. "I owe your girl Chanté."

Kit blinked her tears back, resisting the urge to curl up in his lap. "Don't tell her. She's been eyeing a pair of Choos."

Brick leaned down to help Grim up, and they made for the front of the club. He staggered against the massive brother as Stitch pulled one of the street level doors open and the midday sun blared in.

The van was double-parked, right up front. They made their way to it, and Kit gave a sigh of relief, happy to be—

The doors behind them exploded outward.

A wave of intense heat seared across her back, blowing her forward. She hit hard, face in the gutter, ears ringing with the muted sound of alarms going off, everything shrouded in glittering gray. The hell had just happened?!

Something was wrong with her wrist, her leg... her vision swam...

Oh hell, no. Don't you dare pass out! Move your ass! You can't stay here!

Kit shook her head, distant sirens pricking through her fog. Move. Right. That. She went to push herself up and screamed, hand grinding down on pebbled glass. Kit cradled her arms to her chest—

"Got her!"

A man in leather with a bandana over his face was at her side. "Shit, Grim's gonna fucking kill us..." He ripped the piece of cloth off his face and tied it around her thigh. Wrench. She knew that dude. He'd said shit about Chanté—

Chanté.

Oh, sweet baby Jesus, no—Kit struggled against him as he picked her up.

Chanté, she had to see if—oh God, what if—

A scream tore from her throat.

"Fuck, I'm sorry, I know it hurts, but we gotta go—"

"Chanté! No! Chanté's in there!"

Doc was leaning out the back of the van and Wrench handed Kit over. Bitch wrapped a blanket around her like a straitjacket. The doors slammed, and tires squealed.

"No! We gotta go back! We gotta go back!" Kit sobbed, her struggles weakening against the arms banding her to be still.

Doc let her go and crouched in front of her. "Calm down. We can't go back. Feds are gonna be all over this shit, and the timing of when you came out of there is fucked. No way in hell we'll make it across the bridges before they close them down. Stitch needs that address—"

"Where's Grim? I want Grim!"

"Christ, I said calm the fuck down! That gash on your leg opens up anymore, you're gonna bleed out! Grim's right fucking here. Blast KO'd him—"

Kit froze. "What? Is he okay?"

Doc snorted. "Won't know till he wakes up, but the bastard doesn't have a scratch on him. He's gonna be fucking pissed you do. Now what's the Goddamned address?"

"West 25th street. Go to the Arts Tower," she mumbled, picking out his inert form in the gloom of the van, and numb at the thought of losing him and Chanté.

Stop. You don't know that.

Doc's brows knit. "Chelsea's vamp territory..."

"And Kit's Grim's queen," Stitch snapped from the front seat. "She says that's where we go, that's where we go."

A loaded silence sucked the air from Kit's lungs, Doc's eyes on her intent.

"Yeah. His queen," she grumbled, turning away and grabbing a med kit. "Lemme look at that leg."

Kit leaned against the van's wall while Doc cut away her jeans. She'd pulled on a headlamp and frowned as it lit the wound.

It was bad.

She grabbed a road burn kit from her bag. "I gotta get all the glass out before I can stitch it. That hand looks like shit, too. This is gonna hurt like hell, but it's full of funk."

It more than hurt. Doc was nothing if not thorough. She opened up a suture kit just as they hit a pothole. Kit winced, blinking back tears.

"Can't you fucking drive around those?" Doc yelled at Stitch, inspecting a wicked little needle.

"Should'a seen the one I missed," he muttered. "Tower's just ahead. Any ideas where to park? Streets is fucking mobbed."

Yeah, on a day like this? Galleries would be packed.

"Alley's on the south side, there's a loading dock. They'll know me and will let us up." She hoped. Doc tied off the first suture and started on the next. Kit's stomach roiled. What if she'd misunderstood what Mr. Asorav had said, and they didn't? Nope. Wasn't gonna think about that.

Stitch swore at multiple someones to get out of his way, the van creeping down the block before making a sharp turn into the alley. He backed it up to the loading dock, motorcycles rumbling alongside. Doc had finished wrapping up her leg before the van doors opened. Kit blinked as Deuce climbed in to pick her up bridal-style, then clambered out the back.

The dock was deserted. Crap. There was usually a guy on duty out here…

Stitch ran a hand down his face. "Now what, kid?"

As she took a breath to say she didn't know, the loading dock's bay door rumbled upward.

Mr. Asorav stood in the shadows, surrounded by armed men, cradling Cecelia in his arms. The Pomeranian gave a happy yip, and he tutted her, his long finger booping her nose. "Now, my dear, you are all our guests."

CHAPTER TWELVE

GRIM'S consciousness floated in a sea of pain. Snippets of memory brushing against him like flotsam, then drifting away, others latching on and dragging him down into the inky abyss. Deep sea monsters coming to surface after Chanté's spell had disturbed their slumber…

"Hold!"

Reaper's alpha command cut through him, freezing Grim's finger on the trigger mid-pull.

Fight him, you furry fuck!

—cowering—

A bead of sweat dripped from the tip of Grim's nose. He'd had him. He'd fucking had Reaper, and his Goddamned pussy-ass cat—

Silver glinted at the corner of Grim's eye, pricking at his cheek.

Shiv.

"Think the ladies will like him as much with an eye patch?"

Reaper laughed. "An eye for an eye does appeal, but that pretty face and what's between his legs is what sells the package. Rest of him, though? Think our boy here needs a reminder where he come from."

Grapple growled from beside Clay's lifeless body, kicking it aside and lumbering over.

Shiv gave him a little bow and plucked the gun from Grim's hand. "No, I wouldn't dream of depriving you of the pleasure."

Grapple grunted, and his meaty fist drove into Grim's gut, exploding the breath from him and buckling him forward—

Reaper tsked. "Looks like he done forgot how this works. Shiv, lash the pussy up."

Silver chimed and Grim's wrists were encircled with tight bands. He bit back a scream, the spikes on their inner surface puncturing his flesh, the cold seep of their poison burning into his blood—

They hung him from the rafters. Shiv laughing as Grapple beat him, then taking a turn.

It went on for hours? Minutes? An eternity of blackened and bloodied moments.

His shoulders ached, hands numb, his dead weight slowly cutting off his air supply.

Darkness pricked his vision.

And then he fell.

Blood rushed back into his limbs, forcing him to feel, jolting him back to consciousness with a pain-racked gasp.

Reaper's boots crouched before him. His hand snatched a hank of Grim's hair, ripping his head back. Fingers jammed into his mouth, the coppery tang of blood and the iron of viscera coating his tongue. Grim's stomach spasmed, his busted ribs grinding and shooting agony through him.

Motherfucker had fed him Clay.

"But he was pierced for our transgressions, he was crushed for our iniquities. The punishment that brought us peace—" Reaper snarled, his fetid breath hot on Grim's face, then shoved him away, standing and raising his hands like he was at a revival. "—was on him. And by his wounds—We are healed."

"Amen." Shiv snickered, pausing as he crossed himself. Voices came from outside the club. His eyes flicked to the main doors, the chain wrapped through them rattling. "Believe that's our cue."

Reaper's lips pursed, attention still focused on Grim. "Destiny is nigh, boy. When it calls, you done best pick up the phone..."

Grim whimpered, fear a tight tentacle around him—

Sharp teeth rent it from his consciousness, pulling him away and drawing him close.

—heal—

He sank into his cat's presence, and darkness covered them.

———

Kit sat on the penthouse balcony, the last rays of the sun dipping below the skyline. Cecelia shivered on her lap as Kit's fingers stroked through the dog's fluffy fur. For once, the small creature wasn't much comfort. Inside, Stitch, Doc, and the rest of the crew sat around Mr. Asorav's great table speaking in hushed tones.

None of them had removed their weapons, and they'd barely looked at her.

The news played on the flat screen dominating the wall behind them, the day's events being hashed out ad nauseam.

A bomb had ripped through the club. Emergency personnel were still looking for survivors. As of yet, none had been found, and her texts to Chanté remained unanswered.

Kit swiped a tear away with the back of her bandaged hand. The other lay cradled in a splint. Doc had been truthful about Grim getting out of the destruction unscathed, but he remained unconscious.

Over the city, the sun winked out behind the buildings.

"Ah, there she is. I should have known Cecelia would be keeping you company," Mr. Asorav said a breath later. "But you'll catch a chill if you stay out here much longer. Tell me, is the fellowship inside not to your liking?" He pulled at the creases of his slacks and sat in a chair across from her with a wry smile. "I can't say that I'd blame you."

"Grim's crew doesn't trust you, or me now, because I

brought them here," she murmured, seeing their betrayed glares from the corner of her eye. "Did you really have to point all those guns at them?"

He shrugged. "Seemed the most expedient way to garner their compliance. You're being sought by both the human authorities and Reaper's men. Altering traffic cams is one thing, tracking down every eyewitness is quite another."

Kit bit her lip, fingers still smoothing through Cecelia's fur. "I don't understand why you're helping us."

"Not them. *You.*"

"Mr. Asorav, I walk your dog. I don't think that justifies—"

"Did you ever stop to wonder why, out of every professional service this city has to offer, I personally called a number from a flyer taped up at a shitty deli in Queens?"

Kit opened her mouth and then snapped it shut. Minelli's wasn't a shitty deli, but he had a point, and idiot that she was, she'd just chalked it up to luck.

"Many years ago, Claymore James provided my Queen with a service. In exchange, he asked for us to aid you, should there come a time you require it." His lips quirked at her shock. "I'll admit I felt the same. Why would he waste a favor of the magnitude he was owed on a half-breed he had no relation to? Especially considering the hell he'd left his own son to rot in."

The vamp crossed his ankle over his knee, getting comfortable. "It intrigued me, and when the opportunity presented itself to discover what Claymore was so set on protecting..." He shrugged. "Now I know."

Kit's mouth was dry, her heart thudding in her ears. "Now you know what?"

"To each paranormal sect there can be only one true queen, Katherine. The font from which their power flows. And despite your current affliction with humanity, for the shifters, you are it, or will be, once you embrace your dual nature. That's not distrust in their gazes, it's disbelief. They feel it. The pull to protect you, and I can't fault them for not knowing what to make of it after all this time. It's been over a century since a true queen was born in their midst, and even longer since a princess has transitioned."

Her brow furrowed, abruptly very interested in Cecelia's rhinestone collar. "I don't understand—"

"No, but you will. Aryanna has requested your presence on the morrow," he said, lighting a long thin cheroot.

"Aryanna?"

A sour smile flit across his lips, smoke curling from his nostrils. "The vampire queen. She's eager to meet the shifter princess she's sworn to protect. I must say the irony of her position is delicious, considering she issued the kill order on the last one…"

Kit bit at her lip, not liking the sound of that. Mr. Asorav was okay for a vamp, but the rest of them were sketchy as hell. And what was up with calling her a princess? Reaper had done it too… right before he spat in her mouth to "speed up destiny."

Her stomach roiled, and she felt like she was gonna be sick. She stood, passing Cecelia to Mr. Asorav.

He took the small dog with a frown. "Something troubling you?"

"Claymore… my father… they both knew about this?"

Mr. Asorav scowled. "Reaper Ells knows entirely too much about a great many things, and as for Claymore James…" A smile flit across his face. "He had a gift for strategy like none other. One of the few men I've considered a worthy opponent."

Kit nodded dumbly, and slipped back inside, her thoughts a manic jumble of *What the fuck?*

The crew at the table went silent as she passed, her footfalls lost in the thick Persian carpeting running the length of the halls. Artwork blurred as she passed, her eyes burning. Kit paused at the door of Grim's room, swallowing the lump in her throat before pushing it open.

Moonlight dappled the room beyond, tinted amber by the thick windows. The bed lay in shadow. Kit's arms hugged her waist. Just wanting, needing… Goddamn it, she just wanted someone to fucking hold her! She dashed a hand across her eyes, stumbling to the bed, trying to keep everything in that wanted to burst free—

And Grim was gone.

Her eyes snapped to the bathroom, but it was as empty as the bed. Had he left her? She put a trembling hand to the rumpled covers. What if he'd—No… not—

A solid weight pressed into the small of her back with a chuff, and the distinct musk of cat surrounded her. The small hairs on her nape rose. "G-Grim?"

Another push, this one enough to test her balance, and the strong impression of "No."

Slowly, she turned.

A mountain lion lowered itself to its haunches, its gaze level with her throat. It chuffed again, pressing its head to her breast. That burning want rose up in her, the something she'd shoved down deep. Unabashed, tears slid down her cheeks, her fingers sinking into the softness below its jaw. Feeling the dichotomy of gentle power.

The yearning for something she'd never known. Never wanted.

Was this destiny?

Her heart hardened. No, it was rage.

Claymore, Reaper… one had tried to keep her from it, from this, from who she was, and the other had thrown her into the deep end, laughing. Neither cared about what she wanted.

What did she want?

The lion's head butted against her again, an ear turning back as he rubbed his face against her. God, he was massive, a tawny silver in the tinted light, the dark markings on his face outlining its contours like a skull. Kit shivered. Mountain lion, puma, cougar... *a rose by another name...* but Grim... no —Darke—he was why the natives called them ghost cats.

His midnight-tipped tail flicked against the carpet, eyes outlined in heavy black, glinting with eye-shine. She gazed into his oval pupils, their shape softer than when he fought with Grim, and an overwhelming sense of loss and loneliness washed over her.

It mirrored the acid ache of her mother's absence, of Chanté's unreturned texts, and even the void of Claymore's heavy-handedness. She was alone.

Kit dropped to her knees, pressing herself against the short, thick fur of Darke's chest, the feel of it so right... He snuffed at her hair, nosing it aside, his tongue rasping against her cheek. She pulled back to meet his gaze. "Is he okay?"

Static like bees crept over her consciousness, and a feeling... *He'll be fine, Kit. Darke's got it handled, and until then, we got you, girl.*

Her eyes pinched closed, a sob catching in her throat. That voice... God, she was so stupid...

Mmm... let's go with willfully ignorant and stubborn as hell. That's gotta change, along with this two-legged bullshit, and Daddy dearest's deposit ain't done dick in that department.

Kit's hand rose to her throat. Shit, the change...

Darke yawned, fangs white and glistening, his maw an endless void. Behind him, the moon had risen, peeking from beyond the clouds gathered on the horizon.

Her cat was right. She hadn't changed. But everything else had.

Thank you so much for reading
Grimdarke

Please consider leaving a rating to let other readers know
what you think of the book

Keep Reading for a FREE Mayhem novella prequel

NEXT IN THE SERIES

DARKER

———

SHADES of the past tore through the consciousness Darke shared with his man, threatening to swallow Grim whole. He fought against their poisoned bite, but the witch's spell had weakened the big cat's skin-brother and freed the memories from their fetters. They lashed at Grim with inky black tentacles of torment. His agonized screams rose within the crescendoing squall, clambering through their split psyche. A growl welled in Darke's chest, ruff bristling at their assault.

—*Mine!*— he snarled, lunging into the fray. Sharp claws and teeth rent the shadowed memories of the bad time from his man, scattering them back into the depths of their mind. Grim was his. Him. A self separate, yet one. His skin-brother. Darke nuzzled him close, tongue rasping over Grim's flickering light.

—*heal*—

Kit... his man whimpered, curling into a ball. His light dimmed, giving up control of their form to the big cat.

—*ours*— Darke rumbled, shifting their body and sending Grim what strength he could. Fur sprouted, limbs cracking and reforming. Two legs became four, and a tawny grey mountain lion lay sprawled on the bed where the others had lain his man to recover.

Within, his skin-brother's light strengthened, its low glow holding steady.

Darke ran a paw over his face, licking at his pad. He sneezed at the scent of old blood, the room thick with the patina of its tang and the decaying musk of the undead. A low growl rumbled in his chest, his pupils dilating to take in the room's blend of muted color.

Heavy furniture dominated the space, its angles stark amidst the gloom. Tendrils of age and linseed seeped from the wood to twine with the rest of the civilized rot assaulting his nose. He pushed off the bed, padding across the thick carpet. His shadow greyed the fingers of scant moonlight streaming in from long, amber-tinted windows.

Darke paused, his lip curling over his canines, disdainfully eyeing the city spread out below him before turning his face to the bulbous moon.

Had Grim's female changed and released her animal?

Clay's cat had promised Darke a mate. Teased him with her scent, captured within weft of the afghan on Grim's bed. The desperate longing it evoked proved the connection. The tip of Darke's tail twitched. He'd trusted it would be so. Waited for so long. Too long. Kit's scent matched. That meant the beast within her was his, and sensing his mate within the two-legged female his skin-brother coddled without being able to claim her was torture.

Darke chuffed his frustration, pacing the breadth of the room, eyes narrowed at the heavy oaken door leading out. Beyond it, faint voices pricked at his ears. Part of his skin-brother's pride was near. Darke growled at the snippets of the MC's inner cats' near unintelligible murmuring punctuating the two-legged babble. That he could understand their stupid yapping better than his own brethren's yowls irked.

A pang of loneliness shot through Darke's chest. He missed Clay. When his father's inner lion had spoken, his deep rumble was clarion. The lynxes out there? Rowels and hissing, Darke could pick out maybe one hard-won word in six, and they couldn't understand him at all. It had been the same with his littermates, Grapple and Shiv, leaving Darke to rely on instinct when forced to interact.

It got him in trouble. Lynxes were shady and two-leggers lied. Said things they didn't mean, then hurt you. Clay had been different, but he was dead while his murderer walked free.

Reaper.

Darke shivered, ears flicking back and his pupils dilating, remembering the bad time. The man that called himself their uncle needed to die, and Grapple and Shiv with him.

Darke's temper spiked, his tail swishing. Keenly feeling the loss locked within his mind again, in this stinking place of undead. His skin-brother shared his sorrow at their father's murder, but not Darke's isolation.

And now Grim had left him, too.

Darke shouldered through another door into a smaller room lined with tile. It smelled faintly of excrement and strongly of fabricated pine, the water in the bowl stale and chemical-laced. Darke shook droplets from his maw and chuffed his distaste, returning to the window —

Soft footfalls approached from the beyond the oaken door.

Darke slunk into the deep shadow of an armoire as the heavy slab canted open, then closed. Kit limped to the center of the room, favoring a leg. Her arm was splinted, and a hand bandaged in gauze. A ruddy stain marred its whiteness. She wrapped her damaged limbs around herself with a low sob, the scent of fresh blood perfuming the air as she moved. Darke's nostrils flared at that thread of wrongness twining within the delicate tendrils of citrus, cinnamon, and female musk.

His mate was presenting as wounded prey.

Darke bit back the growl building in his chest, fury pounding through his temples. His claws extended and retracted from the carpet's thick pile. Hale, she'd be a tempting prize for any predator. Injured... He was going to kill—

No. Darke's ears flattened against his skull. His man would think before spilling blood.

But Grim thought too much.

Kit scanned the room, then dashed a hand across her face, stumbling to the bed. Her feet froze at its foot, head snapping to the bathroom, then away. Another low sob eked from her throat, and Darke's ruff stood on end. He would destroy them. Destroy them all. Starting with those that had failed to protect—

—Hey! Boy Vengeance! You really just gonna let her think her think he's gone?—

Darke jumped, fur bristling at the syrupy censure. He backed deeper into the shadows, eyes wide and pulse pounding.

—Aww. Here puss, puss, puss… I don't bite…—

His lip curled over a canine, and a female's mocking laughter flitted through his mind as clearly as the gravelly chuckle of Clay's beast had. Darke's heart leaped, his ears pricking forward, saliva pooling in his maw.

He could understand her.

The beast inside Kit, his promised mate, her words were clear, and she wanted to *play*.

Shit. She wanted to play. He sent his consciousness back to his man, nosing at his inert presence. Shit, shit, shit… what should he do? Act cool. Grim would tell him to act cool. Not to screw this up. Game. *It's a game.* He knew how to play games… Darke buried his eagerness, narrowing his eyes and idly grooming a paw.

—Oh, come on!—

Seconds ticked by, then a frustrated huffing filled his mind.

—Darke, please!—

He lapped between his toes, blood pounding through his skull. Don't fuck this up, don't fuck this up—

—Listen, asshole, Kit's about to lose her—

Darke yawned. —*you are?*—

—*Oooh! I'm about to kick your furry*—

He sent a her visual of exactly how that would turn out. [FURIOUS BLUSHING]

Didn't fuck it up. Pleased at her reaction, Darke licked his chops, sauntering into the moonlight dappling the room as Kit placed a trembling hand upon the bed's rumpled covers. He froze mid-step. This game with his mate aside, Grim had warned him not to frighten Kit, how—?

—*Oh no, don't stop now; rub up on her. Gently. Let her know you're here.*—

Darke swallowed and pressed his brow to the small of Kit's back, chuffing.

She stiffened. Her scent subtly altered, a sour note of fear curdling through it. "G-Grim?"

—*Do it again.*— his mate urged.

Darke butted against Kit, and she swayed, gasping.

—*Now look cute.*—

Teeth bared, his ears flicked back. —*cute?*—

—*laughing*—

Kit slowly turned, and Darke sat, forcing his anxiety to boredom, gaze level with her throat, fighting the urge to lick his lips at the jump of her pulse.

—*Dayum, that ain't cute, but not actively murderous works. How you're even finer on four legs...*—

Darke chuffed his pleasure, pressing his head to Kit's breast and greeting his mate within. Her fingers sank into the soft fur below his jaw, and he leaned into her touch—

Salt tinged the air, moisture staining Kit's cheeks. Her fingers stiffened, and her expression went hard.

Had he done something wrong? Darke tensed, pulse hammering, waiting for the blow of her fist—

—*Shhh, Pussycat. This isn't about you. Give her a minute*— His mate's voice slid through his mind, its caress smoothing the edges of his fear. —*She's straight-up pissed at not having a choice in any of this. Pay attention, 'cause we got issues with over-bearing males. —*

Darke heard the warning, but was pretty sure she didn't mean him. He butted against her, his ear turning back as he rubbed his face beneath her jaw, releasing calming pheromones. Kit's brow furrowed and then she shivered, her body relaxing.

—Mmm… Have I told you you're my new favorite smell? Do that again —

The end of his midnight-tipped tail flicked against the carpet in amusement, and Kit's eyes caught his. His focus stole past their surface to her inner beast staring back at him. Darke's head cocked. It wasn't a challenge, more like…

An overwhelming sense of her loneliness washed over him. His mate knew his pain and shared it. She understood.

Kit dropped to her knees, pressing herself against the short, thick fur of Darke's chest. Her arms encircled his neck, and she gave a contented sigh. He snuffed at her hair, nosing it aside, his tongue rasping against her cheek.

She pulled back to meet his eyes again. "Is he okay?"

His man. Grim. Darke's muzzle crinkled, trying to send out his thoughts to her as he had with Clay, and met resistance. What—?

Darke's heart sank. Reaper's saliva hadn't triggered her change. His mate still wasn't free, and that loneliness he'd felt…

—you hide —

—She's not ready —

He stared at his mate within Kit's eyes, and she looked away at his censure, leaving him caught in Kit's warm chocolate gaze. *—tell her, he heals —*

His mate paused, as if unsure, then, *—He'll be fine, Kit. Darke's got it handled, and until then, we got you, girl —*

Kit's expression pinched closed, and a sob caught in her

throat. Something like the buzzing of bees buffeted against his consciousness.

His mate replied to it, any earlier trepidation replaced with sass. —*Mmm… let's go with willfully ignorant and stubborn as hell. That's gotta change, along with this two-legged bullshit, and daddy dearest's deposit ain't done dick in that department.*—

Kit's hand rose to her throat, eyes wide with panic, but Darke didn't sense any argument from her. He yawned, pleased his mate had taken her two-legged skin-sister well in hand.

His attention returned to the man healing within their shared consciousness. When Grim woke, Darke vowed to do the same. There would be no more waiting.

It was time they claimed their mate.

Want More?

GET YOUR COPY AT: books2read.com/darker

FREE PREQUEL

CATS DON'T ALWAYS *LAND ON THEIR FEET...*

Grimdarke James has got problems. As Vice Prez of the Maw of Mayhem MC, he needs to keep his shit together, but between the constant threat of his inner cat going feral, and Nikki, one of the motorcycle club's mollys, blackmailing him, it's a fine line some days.

Then when an arms deal goes bad, everything goes to hell with it. All fingers point to an old club enemy, a man Grim has reason to both fear and loathe, but the facts don't add up, and everyone is a suspect... including Grim. Faced with the constant threat of Nikki revealing his past and his need to prove himself to the MC, the fragile peace he's made with his cat is threatened.

Out of options and running out of time, Grim sets a bold plan into motion, and the consequences are far more dire than he could have imagined...

Download it at: bit.ly/readmayhem

And for more short stories from the world of the Maw of Mayhem MC, check out:

bit.ly/bitesofmayhem

AK Nevermore

THE DAE DIARIES - URBAN FANTASY WITH SPICE

One Night in Bliss — Flame & Shadow — Air & Darkness — Playing with Fire

THE PRICE OF TALENT - SPICY DYSTOPIAN ROMANCE

*Breeder — Breaker — Destroyer — Binder — Conspirator — Split Overlord — Exile — Dyad **

THE MAW OF MAYHEM - PRN MC EROTIC ROMANCE

*Bites of Mayhem — The Maw of Mayhem — Grimdarke Darker — Kit-Kat — Katherine — Deuce **

STAR-CROSSED CHRONICLES

Weres and Witchery — Wards and Warlocks — Vampires and Vendettas

ANTHOLOGIES & STANDALONES

Secrets We Keep — Sense, Sensibility, & Shifters — Fairytale

**Forthcoming*

ABOUT THE AUTHOR

AK Nevermore is a bestselling author of paranormal, dystopian science fiction, and urban fantasy romance. She enjoys operating heavy machinery, freebases coffee, and gives up sarcasm for Lent every year.

A Jane-of-all-trades, she's a certified chef, restores antiques, and dabbles in beekeeping when she's not reading voraciously or running down the dream in her beat-up camo Chucks.

Unable to ignore the voices in her head, and unwilling to become medicated, she writes full time. Her books explore dark worlds, perversely irreverent and profound, and always entertaining.

Want more Nevermore?
Sign up for her newsletter and never miss a release!

aknevermore.com

www.ingramcontent.com/pod-product-compliance
Lightning Source LLC
Chambersburg PA
CBHW061535310726
48972CB00008B/2467